BOOTS & THE BACHELOR

UGLY STICK SALOON SERIES BOOK #12

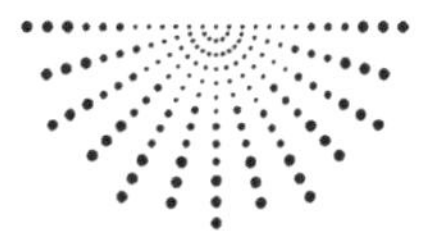

MYLA JACKSON

TWISTED PAGE INC

Enjoy other Ugly Stick Saloon books by Myla Jackson
Ugly Stick Saloon Series
Boots & Chaps (#1)
Boots & Sex Ed (#2)
Boots & Leather (#3)
Boots & Promises (#4)
Boots & Bareback (#5)
Boots & Dirty Tricks (#6)
Boots & Lace (#7)
Boots & Roses (#8)
Boots & Buckles (#9)
Boots & the Wishes (#10)
Boots & Twisters (#11)
Boots & the Bachelor (#12)
Boots & The Rogue (#13)
Boots & The Heartbreaker (#14)
Boots & Wings (#15)

Visit Mylajackson.com for more information
Visit her alter ego Elle James at ellejames.com
Join Elle James and Myla Jackson's Newsletter at
http://ellejames.com/ElleContact.htm

"**Y**ou going to do *what?*" Angus McFarlan slammed his palm on the dining table, too angry to finish the fried chicken, mashed potatoes and gravy his mother had prepared for their dinner.

Maggie, Angus's mother and the matriarch of the McFarlan family, sat at the head of the table where John McFarlan used to sit. She folded her arms. "You heard me. I'm selling the ranch."

Her words hit him again like a sucker punch to the gut.

"Mom, you can't be serious!" Colin, the youngest of the McFarlan brothers, pushed back his chair so fast it fell with a loud crash. "You can't sell the Rafter M Ranch. It's been in the family for over one hundred and fifty years. It's our legacy. Dad would roll over in his grave."

Their mother gave an unladylike snort and tilted her

chin. "I don't see any of my sons giving enough of a damn to see that legacy passed down. And your father would not want me or any of you saddled with it until your dying day only for it to be auctioned off anyway."

Angus sucked in a deep breath and let it out slowly, trying to calm himself before he shouted. His mother's declaration had thrown him for a loop, but it didn't excuse him from disrespecting her. Taking the mature, calm tact, he said in a softer tone, "Don't I work my ass off on this ranch to make it pay? When cattle prices dropped, wasn't I able to redirect our ranching efforts to keep the ranch paying for itself?"

"Angus has put his heart and soul into this place." Colin waved his hand. "He even put his climb up the corporate ladder on hold to take over when Dad died. If he hadn't ramped up the horse breeding and training, we'd have lost the ranch years ago."

"You're only making me more determined. This ranch isn't just a legacy, it's an albatross."

Angus stared at his mother, wondering where was the woman who'd always been optimistic, loving and as hard working as any of her sons? "I don't understand. The ranch is paying for itself and has been making a profit over the last three years. Why sell?"

She pointed a finger at Colin. "For the very reason you say we should keep it."

Colin's eyes widened and then narrowed into a frown. "What reason? You're not making sense, Mom."

"This ranch is a legacy. But what good is a legacy if you don't have anyone to pass it down to?" She folded her napkin and laid it beside her plate of uneaten chicken. "Angus, you and Colin work this ranch, and you work your other jobs as well. Which leaves you exactly how much time off to date, find a nice girl and settle down?" Planting her hands on the table, she stared from one to the other of her sons. "I'll tell you. No time, whatsoever. You can't get a life when you're too busy making a living on this ball and chain of a ranch." She pushed away from the table and stood. "I'm selling the ranch."

Angus stood when his mother did, his thoughts tumbling in his head. "You can't mean it, Mom. This ranch is the McFarlan home."

"Ha!" His mother stamped her foot. "If it's the McFarlan home, why hasn't Brody been back in eight years?"

Colin's lips thinned. "Ask Brody."

Angus shook his head. He wasn't sure why Brody left home eight years ago, but it had something to do with a fight he had with Colin. Colin had never owned up to what started it. "He came for your birthday last year," Angus pointed out.

Again, his mother snorted. "For an entire day. That's it. He doesn't consider this home, and he never stays."

"So? Brody doesn't consider this home, but Angus and I do," Colin said.

Angus changed tactics and tried a little reverse psychology. "Mom, this ranch is yours. Dad left it to you, and you have the right to sell it, if that's what you want."

Colin gasped. "What the hell are you saying, Angus?"

Angus held up his hand. "Dad left the ranch to Mom.

It's hers, not ours."

"You and I both have put our blood and sweat into making this place sustainable," Colin said. "Doesn't that count for anything?"

"Not when the deed is in my name." Their mother stood with her chin tipped upward, her eyes narrowed. "Look, I appreciate that you both came home after your father died and stayed through my surgery and chemotherapy when I had breast cancer, but now it's time for you two to get a life and quit worrying about me or the ranch."

"Mom," Angus said. "We would have left, if we had wanted to, but we don't. We love this place as much as Dad did."

"It's not enough." She raised her hands. "I want my boys married, with kids of their own. As I see it, this ranch is standing in the way of that ever happening. Therefore, I'm selling the ranch."

"So you're serious about the legacy thing?" Angus laughed. "Has Mrs. Reinhardt been bragging about her grandbabies again?"

"No, it's not that." She stopped, chewed on her bottom lip and tilted her head. "Well, a little. Seeing pictures of Jean's grandchildren only brought it home to me that my boys aren't moving on with their lives."

"We're happy with the way we are, Mom." Angus took his mother's hands in his. "Can't you be happy for us?"

She pulled her hands free of his and planted them on her hips. "Angus McFarlan, you're not happy and you don't even know it."

Colin stared up at the ceiling and then back at his mother. "Look at the statistics. Less than fifty percent of marriages last these days."

"Colin has a point," Angus agreed. "Why bother getting married when numbers are against you?"

"Ha!" His mother stamped her foot. "When everyone told you that you couldn't make money training horses, you didn't let that stop you, did you, Angus? I did the research and the *numbers* were against you. But you did it anyway and you made it work. And how did you do that?"

"You know I love horses, and I worked my butt off to make it work."

"Exactly," she said. "And relationships are the same. If you love someone, you have to work hard to make the marriage work. Your father and I fought, didn't we?"

Colin chuckled. "You both gave as good as you got."

"And we never went to bed mad at each other. It took a lot of compromise and work to make our relationship last. Just like with anything worthwhile in life." She nodded toward Colin. "When you started your construction business, you hardly had two nickels to rub together. You worked on building relationships with your subcontractors and with the community. That wasn't easy, was it?"

"No, but that's different."

"No, it's not." Maggie McFarlan shook her head. "You have to feed and nurture a relationship, whether it's business or personal. They don't just happen."

Angus hadn't met a woman worth all the fuss. "Frankly, Mom, I prefer talking to horses than to women. They don't talk back, and they aren't a lot of drama."

His mother's brows shot up. "Dexter, your quarter horse stud, doesn't cause a lot of drama?"

Angus's lips curled upward. "Dexter is special."

His mother rolled her eyes. "And you put up with his tantrums, the many times he breaks through fences or terrorizes the geldings and everything else, because he's *special?*" Her chest rose and fell on a long breath. "A woman can be special too, and worth the effort."

"Dexter generates a lot of money through his stud services," Angus said, hating that he sounded defensive.

Maggie stamped her foot. "Damn it, Angus, there's more to life than money."

"Mom, mom, mom." Colin, ever the charmer, slipped his arm around their mother's shoulders. "You're just upset. Mrs. Reinhardt brags about everything. It's not worth getting your shorts in a twist."

Angus stepped back as the color rose in his mother's cheeks and fire blazed in her eyes. He knew better than to patronize his mother. Colin's usual soothing tactics weren't going to work on her this time. In fact, they appeared to be about to backfire.

Bracing himself, Angus waited for his sweet, kind, rarely angry mother to erupt like a volcano.

She lifted Colin's arm and stepped out from beneath it. "My decision stands. I'm selling the ranch, unless you three McFarlan boys prove to me this ranch is a legacy that *will* have someone to pass on to."

Angus's back straightened, his body stiff. "Smells like an ultimatum to me."

"I don't care if it smells like cow paddies." Angus's mother's fist clenched. "You three boys better get it together and find wives, settle down and have some kids, or this place is gone."

"Three?" Colin frowned. "Brody doesn't even live here."

"Then you better find a way to get him back. I won't go through the rest of my days with one son running away from home for the rest of his life." She spun and marched out of the kitchen.

"She's just pulling our chain, right?" Colin rubbed his chin, staring at the empty doorway.

Angus cringed. Colin had spoken all too soon. Their mother had excellent hearing from clear across the house. Three…two…one…

Their mother reappeared in the doorway. "Here's pulling your chain: I have a real estate broker coming tomorrow to discuss breaking up and selling this ranch, however it has to be done. I'll give you boys one month to fix what's broke between Colin and Brody, get Brody back and get married. If you can't do that in one month, I'm listing this place and entertaining all offers."

"One month!" Angus thundered. "How can you expect us to meet and marry a woman in one month? It's insane."

"Okay, I'll give you two. But no more. And it's all or none. This deal includes your brother Brody."

"But—" Colin started.

Their mother held up her hand. "It's not up for negotiation." She spun, took one step and spun back. "Oh, and just to make it clear, I'm done cooking, cleaning and running your errands. If you want clean laundry or a cooked meal, do it yourself. I've made it far too easy on you boys. It's time you grew up, and, for that matter, it's time I got a life of my own."

Angus crossed his arms. "And where are we supposed to meet these women you want us to marry? Most of the ones I know are married or taken."

His mother smiled. "You boys are in luck. It's ladies' night at the Ugly Stick Saloon. There will be a whole herd of women. It's a good start and a good way to prove you're taking me seriously. I suggest you both shower, put on your best boots and get over there."

"You can't threaten us to get married," Colin grumbled.

Their mother's eyes narrowed. "No, but I can sell the ranch. And I will."

"I HAVEN'T BEEN to the Ugly Stick Saloon in seven years." Gwendolyn Graves glanced around the bar's interior crammed full of women. "I guarantee I've never seen it this packed."

Mona Daley laughed. "This is the Annual Cowboy Auction. The event brings in women from all over the state, and even Oklahoma and Arkansas. The money raised is always for a good cause and we have a ball. You remember Bunny Leigh, don't you?"

"I do." Gwen smiled. "She loved arranging flowers. How is she doing? If I remember correctly, she was just getting married."

Mona's lips curved upward. "The good news is that

she owns her own flower shop now." She frowned. "The bad news is that marriage didn't last. But then it's good news." Mona waved her hand. "Sounds confusing, but she ditched the cheating bastard, bought herself two handsome cowboys at one of these cowboy auctions, and is now living happily with both of them."

Gwendolyn blinked. "My goodness. I don't know whether to offer her my condolences or congratulations."

"Congratulations. She's never been more sexually satisfied."

Nodding, Gwen said, "Wow. Two cowboys?"

"Two of the hottest cowboys in the tricounty area. And she's over-the-moon happy."

"Are *they* happy?" Gwen's core tightened at the thought of having two men to satisfy her every sexual desire. Hell, she'd be happy to have just one.

"The guys have always been really close. Sharing Bunny came natural. What about you?" Mona waved her mug of beer at Gwendolyn. "Have you finally started dating? We have to do a better job of keeping in touch. It's not like you're halfway around the world. You're only in Dallas. Once a year get-togethers aren't nearly enough."

"I know." Gwen tucked a stray strand of hair behind her ear. "You knew I took over as CEO of the small cosmetics company I worked for, didn't you?"

"Honey, you didn't just take over as CEO, you bought the damned company." Mona leaned over and hugged her. "I read about it in the newspaper. Congrat-ulations."

Her cheeks warmed. "Thank you. But owning your own company is very time-consuming. Especially when you're trying to expand and grow it as much as I have. I haven't had time to breathe for the past year. I've gone from ten employees to over forty."

Mona whistled. "I don't know how you do it. I can barely manage my shop and I'm the only one working there."

Gwen laid a hand on her friend's arm. "Honey, small can be so much easier. I don't have time for anything but work."

"What about your love life?"

With a snort, Gwen shook her head. "No time." And, sadly, no desire.

"That summer you came home from college, I thought for sure you and Angus McFarlan were a thing." Mona tilted her head. "What happened with that?"

"I went back to college." Gwen shrugged. "He never contacted me."

"That's too bad. You two seemed perfect together."

She'd thought so too. On their last date, he'd taken her to the top of a hill on the Rafter M Ranch in his pickup. They'd stretched out a blanket on the grass, made love beneath a star-studded Texas sky and fallen asleep in each other's arms. In the middle of the night, she'd woken beside him, so filled with love and longing. The last thing she wanted to do was return to College Station to finish her degree.

Had he asked her to marry him that night, she'd have said yes and chucked college.

But he hadn't. Angus had told her how important it

was for her to get her education, and that he understood she had to leave. Feeling optimistic that he'd wait for her, she'd tucked a letter in the back pocket of his jeans, telling him the things she'd been too shy to say out loud. She loved him and hoped he'd wait for her. At the bottom, she'd given him her phone number and address in College Station and told him to call her if he got the chance.

Two months passed and he didn't write, call or visit. At Christmas when she would normally have gone home for the holidays, her parents announced they'd sold the house, bought a motor home and would be spending the winter in Florida.

Angus hadn't contacted her by Christmas and, with no family left in Temptation, she had no reason to return.

"How's Dalton doing in his new school?" Mona's question pulled her back to the present. "What is he, six now?"

"He'll be six soon." Her son was the center of Gwen's world. A child born out of stupid sex and a quickie marriage in Vegas, Dalton was the farthest thing from a mistake. He was her everything. "Dalton is the perfect son. He's respectful, loving, kind to animals and smart as a whip."

Mona clapped her hands. "And I bet Grant is having a ball as we speak. You should have seen him going through his old sports stuff from his high school days when I told him you were coming."

"I didn't come down from Dallas to stick Grant with babysitting." Gwen sighed. "I needed a break from work and the city, and it's been far too long since I came to visit you here in Temptation."

"Damn right it has. Seven years to be exact. Hell, since your parents sold out and moved to Florida."

"I miss this place."

"I miss you." Mona set her beer mug on the bar and hugged her friend. "I'm glad I talked you into girls' night out."

"I am too. It's been a while since I've had a night out. Much as I love my son, it's nice to have a break."

Mona settled back on her barstool and drank a swallow of beer. "So you traveled all the way to Temptation just to see me?"

"I needed to talk to someone who wasn't from the city. Someone down-to-earth."

Mona's brows crinkled. "That doesn't sound sexy at all. You're making me feel like my grandmother."

Gwen laughed. "Not at all. You're young, vibrant and..." her lips twisted as she thought how to phrase her words, "...well, everything I feel like I've lost in myself."

"What?" Mona leaned back. "Look at you. You're a freakin' knockout. I can't even offer to do your hair. You must have some high-dollar stylist at your beck and call."

Heat rushed up in her cheeks. "Yeah. I do. But that's not why I came. I need advice."

"You're the owner of a growing company. What would I know about the world you don't know already?"

"I have Dalton in a good school. They wear uniforms

every day and they have high academic standards. He's almost six, but he's reading at a fourth-grade level already."

"And that's a problem?" Mona's brow scrunched. "I don't see a problem."

"I'm a single mom, raising a son. I teach him right from wrong, to be kind to others and help him with his homework. I'm doing the best I can." Gwen twisted her hands together.

Mona smiled across her beer. "What child needs more than that?"

"*He* does. He's a good kid, but I can't be everything to him." Gwen sighed. "He needs a male role model. One he can look up to. A man who can teach him what it takes to be a good man."

Mona nodded. "You're smart, what is it you can't do that a man could?"

Gwen raised a finger. "For one, I can't throw a baseball to save my life. I'm even worse at football. I admit, I'm hopeless when it comes to sports."

"So?" Mona laughed. "Sign him up for a community team. I'm sure Dallas has loads of them."

"They do, but it's not just that." Gwen raised a second finger. "He needs to know how to defend himself."

"Put him in a martial arts class."

"I could do that, but it's more than classes and sports. He needs a role model, someone he can talk to and ask guy questions."

Mona gave her a pointed look. "Then why aren't you dating? If you found a man you could love, he could provide Dalton with that male role model you think he needs."

"That's like interviewing men for a position as my son's father." Gwen grimaced. "I wouldn't do that to the man, and I wouldn't want to marry a man I don't love just to give Dalton a dad."

"Give yourself a break, sweetie. You might find the perfect guy you and Dalton could both love."

Gwen shook her head. "It's too much to ask a guy to take on a ready-made family. I've given up on marriage and dating until Dalton is grown and on his own."

"Wow, that's harsh."

"It's reality. Besides, I don't have time for a man in my life."

"I think you protest too much." Mona grinned. "When was the last time you got laid?"

Gwen gasped. "Mona!"

Her friend shrugged. "A woman has needs, just like a man."

"We were talking about my son. Not me."

"Fine. Have it your way." Mona chugged the last of her beer and set it on the counter. "But I think you need a man to give you some hot, dirty sex to get your female juices flowing again. Your vagina is like any other muscle. It needs to be exercised or it shrivels up from lack of use."

Gwen clapped both hands to her burning cheeks. "Mona, please. Change the subject. You're embarrassing me." And making her hot just thinking about exercising her woman parts. God, it had been far too long since she'd had a man in her bed and her vibrator just wasn't getting her off anymore.

Mona pushed her mug toward Libby, the bartender. "Can you set us up with a couple of tequila shots?"

Libby plopped two shot glasses on the counter and spilled tequila into them, then she sliced a lime into quarters and set them in a glass beside the tequila shots. "Want salt with that?"

"Damn right," Mona said.

Libby plunked a shaker of salt beside the tequila and limes. "Let me know when you need a refill."

Mona lifted a shot glass. "You remember how, right? It's as easy as one, two, three. Salt." She licked the curve in her hand between her thumb and forefinger, shook salt over where she'd licked and then sucked the salt off her hand. "Tequila." Mona upended her shot glass, downing the tequila in one swallow. "Lime." Jamming the lime in her mouth, she bit into the fruit, her face puckering. "Whew! That burns so good." She nodded toward the other shot glass. "Your turn."

Gwen hadn't done tequila shots since college and stared at the shot glass skeptically. Then she shrugged and performed the same routine—salt, tequila, lime— downing the liquid in one fiery gulp.

The alcohol burned down her throat all the way to her stomach, shooting flames outward to her extremities.

After a moment, the alcohol settled in, numbing the back of her throat first, then her tongue and finally the tips of her fingers.

"Have you thought about getting Dalton into a mentoring program?"

"No, I hadn't thought about that," she said, her tongue feeling heavy and a bit slow. "How would I know I'd be getting a good one?"

"You could screen them." Mona glanced around the saloon at the laughing, giggling women. "Hell, Gwen, buy a cowboy tonight. Audrey only invites the best to be auctioned. They have to be polite, with no criminal record, and an all-around good guy, or she wouldn't let them be auctioned off."

Heat filled Gwen's cheeks. "I couldn't do that. These men are expecting to go on a date with a *woman*. Not a woman and her son."

"I bet they wouldn't mind. That would give you a jump start with that male role model you want. He might even teach Dalton how to ride."

The thought held merit. Dalton had been pestering her for riding lessons. Who better to teach him than a cowboy? She could arrange to have the dates at a local riding stable. Dalton and the cowboy could ride while she watched from the other side of the fence.

"And you might find that you like the cowboy, fall in love and the three of you will live happily ever after." Mona hopped off her stool. "I'll be right back."

"Where are you going?" Gwendolyn had met Audrey Anderson, the owner, and Libby, the bartender, but she didn't know anyone else in the crowded room.

Mona waved a hand as she disappeared into the crowd.

"Can I get you another drink?" Libby asked.

Gwen stared down at the empty shot glass, warmth still floating through her, and smiled. "Yes, please." Seven summers ago, Angus had taught her an appreciation for tequila right there in the Ugly Stick Saloon. She glanced around, half hoping to see the man who'd ruined her for any other man. He'd set the bar too high for any of the men she'd dated, and they never quite rose to that level.

Angus was kindhearted, loved his family, kept his promises, and he was good with animals. Not to mention, he was an excellent lover. Her thighs tingled. She tried to count it off as the tequila still working its way through her system, but she knew that would be a lie.

The memories of Angus lying between her legs, making sweet love to her in the bed of his pickup, on the sweet-scented prairie grass and in the secluded hunter's cabin on a far corner of the Rafter M Ranch, were never far from her mind.

He was the kind of man she wanted as a role model for her son. A man's man, who knew how to treat a woman. Then again, he'd failed in one category. He'd never come after her.

She'd learned a valuable lesson with Angus McFarlan. Don't fall in love with a cowboy. Apparently, she'd been a summer fling to him. Once she'd gone, she was out of sight and out of the man's mind.

Mona returned bearing a paddle with a number on it.

"What's that?" Gwen asked.

"What does it look like?" Mona held it out.

Gwen shook her head and raised her hands. "Oh no. I'm not going there."

"Yes. You are." Mona took Gwen's hand and placed the paddle in her palm. "You do have a sizeable chunk of money you really want to go to the women's shelter, don't you?"

"I'll make a donation. I don't need a date with a cowboy to do that."

"Well, the only cowboys who will be here tonight are the ones going up for bid. If you want one to help you out with Dalton, you'll have to up the ante and bid for him."

Her stomach burbled and her chest tightened. "I can't." Despite her protest, a tingle of anticipation rippled through her.

"You're a high-powered business owner with more balls than most men I know."

"Exactly." Gwen nodded, pushing aside the insane thought of owning a cowboy. "I don't need to buy a cowboy to prove it."

"Honey. Yes. You. Do." Mona curled Gwen's fingers around the paddle. "Bring on the cowboys!" she yelled. "We're gonna ride one tonight!"

Libby stood behind the bar, holding the tequila bottle up for Gwen to see. "More?"

"Yeah, I guess."

The bartender tipped the tequila into her shot glass. "Will that be all?"

Gwen rolled her eyes, her stomach pitching. "Make it a double. I think I'm buying a cowboy tonight."

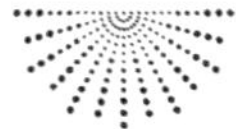

CHAPTER TWO

Angus climbed down from his truck, plunked his cowboy hat on his head and cringed at the loud music shaking the tin roof of the Ugly Stick Saloon.

Colin joined him. "You don't think she'll sell the ranch, do you?"

"The ranch is in Mom's name. She can do anything she wants with it." He hoped and prayed she wouldn't sell, but who knew what she would do after the way she'd left them earlier.

A stream of women had lined up at the door to get in.

Colin grinned. "At least she didn't have to twist my arm to come out on ladies' night. It's not that I don't love women; it's just that I love all of them. I always say, why get stuck with one when you can enjoy the lot?" He settled his hat on his head and smiled. "This'll be fun."

Angus's gut tightened as he neared the crowd. It wouldn't be fun for him. "I'm not good at this."

"It's easy. All you have to do is be a good listener. Nod a few times and crack your face every once in a while with a smile." Colin patted Angus's back. "Mom's right. You've spent far too much time with your horses."

"I like horses," Angus grumbled.

"And you don't like women?" Colin puffed out his chest. "A man has needs."

Angus shrugged. "I get my needs satisfied with a widow woman in Amarillo, once a month when I go to the horse auction. I get what I want, she gets what she wants, no strings. It's perfect."

Colin shook his head. "Angus, big brother, you really do need to get a life."

Angus glared at his brother. "And you're much better? You're with a different woman every week? How's that better? At that rate, you'll never marry and have kids. Mom wants you to settle down with one woman, not a harem."

"I haven't met the one woman I want to spend the rest of my life with. How does Mom expect me find her in two months when I've been dating women for the past eight years and have yet to even narrow it down to twenty?"

As they neared the bar, the woman at the back of the line waiting to get in spotted them and squealed and shouted, "Here come the cowboys!"

The rest of the women turned and made the same screeching noise as the first. As one, the crowd of females rushed toward them, feral looks blazing from their eyes.

Angus would have turned and run if Colin hadn't hooked his arm.

"You should see your face." Colin laughed out loud. "Come on, don't be chicken. They're just a bunch of women."

"But they're eyeing us like sides of beef."

"Enjoy it!" Colin let the ladies grab his hands and usher him through to the door.

Angus was swept along behind him and practically shoved through the entrance into the Ugly Stick Saloon.

The crowd of ladies inside was even wilder than the one outside. Angus and Colin were pushed, shoved and pinched as they inched through the mob to the bar.

"I can't do this," Angus said again as his ass was pinched and some really daring woman grabbed his package. "Hey!"

The woman winked. "Just testing the goods." She turned to her friend. "That one's mine."

"Move aside, girls." Audrey Anderson, five months pregnant and barely showing, waded through the crowd toward them, hooked Colin's arm and then Angus's. "Let them through. Give these fine cowboys some air to breathe." She chuckled and led them toward the bar and two empty stools. "Have a seat, gentlemen. The fun begins in a few minutes. What can I get you? The drinks are on the house for the cowboys tonight."

"Whiskey. Make it a double." Angus needed all the help he could get.

"Angus, when are you going to sell me that quarter

horse stud?" Jackson Gray Wolf was seated on the stool beside Angus. He set down his beer and held out his hand.

Angus took it, glad for a little testosterone in the sea of feminine laughter and rabid glances. "When are you ready to pay an arm and a leg for him?"

"I'm ready. I just sold some stock and made a pile of money. I can afford him."

Angus shook his friend's hand. "Sorry to disappoint, but I'm not in the market to sell him anytime soon. But it's always good to see you, Jackson."

"That's a shame." Jackson turned and shook hands with Colin. "Your mother called to let us know you were on your way. Thanks for coming. Glad to hear she's still cancer-free."

Angus was still angry at his mother's ultimatum, but he couldn't be mad long. The woman had been through so much with her husband's death and then a two-year-long battle with breast cancer. She was tough, but her family meant everything to her. Angus could understand her desire to see them all settled with wives and children of their own. She probably thought she wouldn't be around forever and that they needed someone to see them through hard times.

Angus stared out at the mob of women. Searching for a wife in this insanity wasn't his idea of how to go about doing it.

Jackson grinned. "Feeling outnumbered?"

"You bet." If Angus were prone to panic attacks, he'd swear he was on the verge of one.

Jackson shook his head and ran a hand through his

thick black hair. The man commanded attention with the high cheekbones, strong jaw and piercing eyes of his Kiowa ancestors. "We had two of our cowboys call in sick. With this crowd, it might have caused a riot. When your mother called and said you were coming, I wanted to reach through the phone and hug the woman."

Though Angus loved his mother and was glad her cancer was in remission, he didn't feel much like hugging her. She'd condemned him to a night of screaming females, all wanting to touch him and pinch his ass. Had they no shame? "I'm here for the whiskey." He'd have a couple drinks, maybe a burger from the grill, hang out a while and head home. That ought to appease his mother and maybe she'd calm down and quit the crazy talk.

Sell the Rafter M Ranch? Over his cold, dead body.

He leaned over to Colin and whispered, "How much money you got in the bank?"

"Not enough to buy a three-thousand-acre ranch. And neither do you."

"If we put our savings together—"

"We might have a small down payment. But what bank would loan us the amount it would take to buy three thousand acres of prime range?" Colin shook his head and lifted his glass to his lips. "The odds would be more in our favor of finding a wife in two months than scrounging up a sizeable down payment. And holy hell, think of the monthly mortgage bill that would eat up every bit of profit either one of us could make off that place."

Yup, they were screwed. Angus raised his glass and

downed the whiskey, welcoming the slow burn it made all the way to his belly.

Jackson leaned toward the brothers. "Get ready, they're about to start."

Angus, along with the crowd of women, turned toward the stage where Audrey stood with a microphone in her hand. "Ladies and, er, Ladies!"

The women in the crowd whooped and hollered.

"I want to thank you all for coming out and bringing your hard-earned cash to the Ugly Stick Saloon's Annual Cowboy Auction. This year's proceeds will benefit the county women's shelter."

Another round of whoops and hollers.

Angus nearly slid off his chair and left. Already his ears rang, and he couldn't hear himself think.

"Ha!" Colin laughed. "Trust Mom to make this night interesting."

"Yeah, well, I'm ready to head home." He couldn't understand any man who'd be willing to put himself on display like a prized bull on the auctioneer's block. The man would have to be insane, desperate or have a pair of iron balls.

"You can't go now. We have to see who they suckered into being auctioned off tonight. This'll be a hoot." Colin sat back, a grin on his face, his whiskey in his hand.

Charli Sutton, Connor Mason's fiancée and Audrey's assistant manager of the Ugly Stick Saloon, took the mic from Audrey. She shook back her mane of blond hair and grinned. "Who's ready for some beefcake?"

Angus could swear the noise emitted from all those

women actually lifted the roof of the building. He fought the urge to cover his ears.

"Our first cowboy up for bid has a thirty-two-inch waist, is six feet tall, has black hair and gray eyes. He's offered to escort the winning bidder on two dates to the winner's choice of locations. This handsome cowboy grew up on a ranch, but prefers his horses with wings. Please give it up for the sexy resident flyboy, Jake Maddox!"

Charli stepped aside to the crushing applause as Jake Maddox swaggered out on the stage in jeans, cowboy hat, boots and a blue chambray shirt. Raunchy stripper music played and Jake, whom Angus considered a friend, strutted around the stage, tipped his hat to the crowd of women and winked. Then he unbuttoned his shirt, one button at a time, pulled it off his back and tossed it into the crowd.

Like a shark feeding frenzy, the women fought over the shirt, ripping it to shreds.

Angus couldn't bear to watch his friend's shame as the bidding started and the women holding numbered paddles practically foamed at the mouth in their excitement to win two dates with Jake. Poor bastard.

While the bidding continued, Angus leaned across the counter and held up his glass to get the bartender's attention.

Libby Jones hurried over. "Another whiskey?"

Angus shook his head. The way Colin was knocking back the drinks, someone would have to drive him home. "No. I'm designated driver. Water would be great. And something for a headache, if you have it."

Libby set him up with a glass of iced water and a couple of generic ibuprofen pills. As he chugged them down, the flash of auburn hair at the other end of the bar caught his attention, reminding him of a girl he knew from, hell, how many years ago? Six? Seven?

His pulse leaped and he tried to see her around the other people crowding up to the bar for another drink. It couldn't be the beautiful, carefree college girl he'd fallen for that summer between her junior and senior years of college.

Gwen Graves.

That had been the year his father died. He'd given up his job at the firm in Dallas and returned home to run the ranch.

One day he'd been in Temptation collecting supplies and feed. He'd literally run into her at the diner. He'd gone in for a quick bite to eat. As he left, he'd turned to say goodbye to a friend and opened the door in Gwen's face, knocking her over. When he'd apologized she'd told him he could make it up to her by buying her a milkshake. That had been the beginning of something he'd spent the next seven years trying to forget.

They'd seen each other every day for an entire month. She'd taught him how to two-step at the Ugly Stick Saloon. He'd tried to teach her how to ride a horse western style, but she'd preferred riding double behind him, her arms around his waist.

She'd gone with him out to tend cattle and mend fences, helping him by handing him a hammer and nails. Her smile rivaled the sun, the light smattering of freckles across the bridge of her nose adding to her sweet girl-next-door appeal, and her body…

He could picture her as if it were yesterday. One hot day, they'd gone to the creek to cool off in the natural pool shaded by willow trees. He'd watered the horse and turned to find her standing naked on the rock ledge overlooking the pool's smooth surface.

"Last one in is a rotten egg!" She winked, trotted over to the edge and dove in, swam to the middle and flipped over onto her back, her bare breasts gleaming in the dappled sunlight finding its way through the tree branches. "Feels so good."

To this day, his throat locked up and he fought to swallow at the image of her smooth white breasts tipped with tantalizing rosy areolas, half-submerged in the water, her smile urging him to join her. That particular memory was indelibly etched into his mind.

The woman at the end of the counter only resembled Gwen by the color of her hair.

When he got a better look, he realized it couldn't be her. Her face was perfectly made up and she wore a light-gray business suit. She appeared to be more interested in her conversation with Mona Daley, Temptation's beauty shop owner, than in the bidding war that had begun over Jake.

Angus wondered if the woman in the business suit was single. Then again, he hadn't had much in common with the women he'd met when he'd worked in Dallas at an architectural firm. They'd all been too uptight, wearing narrow pencil skirts and high heels. He'd much rather be with a woman comfortable in jeans and cowboy boots.

Like Gwen.

He sighed.

Ah, Gwen. Timing couldn't have been better or worse. He'd needed her joyous spirit and love of life that summer. His father's death had been a huge blow to the family. Without giving it a second thought, Angus gave up his dreams of being in charge of building incredible skyscrapers, to return to the ranch and help out his grieving mother. With one brother gone, the other in college, it had been up to him to take over.

When Gwen left, Angus had every intention of going after her. But circumstances and his mother's fight with breast cancer put the kibosh on that plan. He couldn't expect Gwen to put her life on hold, waiting for him. She was a young, vibrant woman on the verge of graduating college and starting a new career. He'd only hold her back.

Since that summer, Angus hadn't been interested in any other woman. None of them had Gwen's smile or her beautiful hazel eyes—gold one minute and green the next. The thought of starting all over and putting his heart out there again held no appeal to him. It hurt too much.

"Sold! The two dates with the handsome Jack Maddox go to bidder number 549 for one thousand dollars. Congratulations, and thank you for your donation to the women's shelter."

The women clapped and cheered, patting the winner on the back.

Audrey emerged from the crowd, grinning. "Wasn't that great? One thousand dollars!"

Jackson smiled and pulled her between his knees. "That's great, sweetheart. Shouldn't you be off your feet?"

She cupped his cheek in her palm. "I'm fine. I think the baby likes all this noise. She's been kicking ever since the bidding started."

"*He* will never be one of the cowboys strutting across that stage." Jackson kissed the tip of her nose and caressed her hips.

Audrey ran her fingers through his hair and cupped the back of his neck. "Oh, come on, you've done your share of stripping for the cause."

"I didn't do it on purpose," Jackson protested. "I was *stripped*."

"You say potato. I say tomato." She grabbed his hand and pulled him to his feet, her eyes gleaming wickedly. "Could you help me out in the storeroom? I'm sure there's a box I just can't lift." With a wink to Libby behind the bar, she dragged Jackson away. Although dragged wasn't exactly how he went.

The man looked more than willing to go.

"That's what we need," Colin commented.

"What's that?" Angus asked.

"A relationship like Audrey and Jackson have."

"Those are so few and far between." Angus slid off the stool. "Ready to go?"

Colin's brows wrinkled. "Come on, Angus. Stay. I'm getting a kick out of watching this whole process." He glanced around the room. "I can't wait to see the next schmuck they conned into this."

"Might be worth it if they were auctioning off a cook. With Mom on strike, we're going to suffer."

"Shh. Charli's about to announce the next cowboy." Colin leaned forward, a grin spreading across his face. "Gotta see who will be the next sucker."

"Ladies, this next hunkilicious man is a once-in-a-lifetime opportunity for some lucky woman. He's tall at six feet two inches."

"Ahhh," the crowd sighed as one.

"He's got black hair and amazing gray eyes." Charli dragged it out, spurring their anticipation.

Angus shook his head. Somewhere behind the stage or in the crowd, a cowboy was probably shaking in his boots, dreading the moment his name was announced and he was paraded around the stage like a pony.

"Descended from strong Scottish warlords, he's a true-blue, honest-to-goodness, rough-around-the-edges rancher with big, calloused hands." Charli paused and winked at the women. "You know what that means."

The women screamed and clapped, beer sloshed and laughter followed. Every numbered paddle in the room fluttered.

Colin elbowed Angus in the ribs. "I could swear they're describing you."

Angus leaned forward, his heart stuttering against his ribs. He drew in a breath and held it.

"Ladies, our next offering will be for not one, not two, not three dates with this hunka hunka burnin' love.

The lucky winner gets *four* dates with a man some would call a horse whisperer, a real-life cowboy, boots and all." Charli stared across the room, straight into his eyes. "One of Texas's most eligible bachelors, Angus McFarlan!"

Colin shouted, "Hot damn!" Then he laughed so hard he doubled over, a hand pressed to his side, and fell off his stool.

How could this be? "I didn't sign up for this," Angus said, but wasn't heard over the shouts and catcalls from the hundreds of horny women in the crowd.

Still sputtering, Colin pointed a finger at him. "You should see your face. I can't believe she did this."

"Who?" Angus would like to get his hands around the throat of whoever had played this rotten trick on him.

"Who do you think? Mom!" Colin slapped Angus on the back. "You're in it now. These women won't let you back out."

"Come on up to the stage, Angus." Charli crooked her finger and grinned. "The ladies want to see what they're getting for their money."

Angus turned to run, but was blocked by Greta Sue, the bar's bouncer.

"Come on, cowboy, we'll get you there in one piece." Greta Sue grabbed his hand in her manlike grip and charged forward like a linebacker breaking through the defensive line of an opposing football team.

Angus tried to free his hand, but Greta Sue held tight. Short of hurting her, he had to go along.

Women touched, pinched and kissed his cheeks as

he passed through the crowd. One of them caught hold of his shirt and wouldn't let go. With Greta Sue pulling him one direction and his shirt going the other, the buttons gave, popping one at a time until the last one ripped free of the fabric. The shirt came off as he was pushed and shoved from behind, with Greta Sue leading the charge in the front.

The only good thing about making it to the stage was that Greta Sue released his hand and the women couldn't pinch his ass. Angus stood, glaring at the rabid females, rubbing his butt and wishing he were anywhere but there. The exit seemed so far away. He spun, hoping to duck out the back of the stage, but Greta Sue stood behind him, her arms crossed, feet spread.

He could knock her down and make a run for it, but his mama had taught him better than to hit a woman, no matter how manly she might be. Getting through the crowd to the exit was not even the slimmest possibility.

Charli stood to the side, with that damned silly grin on her face. "What will you give for four dates with this mass of purely masculine muscle?"

Angus closed his eyes and prayed no one would bid. That he'd be allowed to walk free of this huge embarrassment. When he got home, he'd have a long talk with his mother about volunteering him for charity events he had no desire to be a part of.

"Five hundred dollars!" a woman shouted, waving her paddle from the middle of the room.

Angus's hopes for a humiliating but commitment-free escape melted away as the first paddle rose high in the air.

"Do I hear seven-fifty?" Charli prompted.

"Yup!" Another paddle shot into the air.

"One thousand. Do I hear one thousand dollars?" Charli barely got the words out before another paddle rose.

"Me!" the woman cried out.

Angus stared out into the mass of eager female faces. "Ms. Fenton?" Was that the gray-haired librarian he used to visit once a month as a kid?

"That's right, sweetie, I might be old, but I'm not dead." She winked at him. "At least not yet. And I'd like a little beefcake to keep me warm for four delicious dates."

Angus's eyes widened. Holy shit. What was it about a cowboy auction that got the young and old single women to come out of the woodwork and blow their hard-earned cash on a few measly dates?

"Fifteen hundred anyone?" Charli stared around the room.

Angus did too, wondering if anyone would outbid Ms. Fenton and rescue him from four dates with a woman old enough to be his grandmother but with a wicked grin that frankly had Angus quivering in his boots.

The bidding stalled and Angus had to do something to get it going again, or he would be spending the next month taking Old Lady Fenton out to dinner. Not that she wasn't nice and all, but the way she was rubbing her hands together made him as nervous as a cat in a room full of rocking chairs.

Desperation drove him to do something he would never have done in a million years.

Angus tightened his abs and shoved a hand through his thick hair, pausing like the models and weightlifters did to show off the hard-earned six-pack definition across his belly. He hadn't gained those muscles in a weight room. Tossing hay bales and lifting heavy fence posts did that to a man over the years.

God, he felt silly, but the crowd surged forward and eyes widened.

"One thousand going once…" Charli started.

"Fifteen hundred!" The woman who'd shouted was probably in her forties.

Angus nodded. Better. He couldn't expect the younger ladies to have that kind of money. Dating a cougar wouldn't be bad. Hopefully, she wouldn't expect more than the four dates and he'd be done. Free to spend time with his horses.

"Turn around!" another woman shouted.

"Come on, Angus," Charli said. "Turn around and let the women see the whole package."

He frowned at her.

"It's for a good cause," Charli cajoled.

"Come on, Angus," Colin's deep voice called out over the others. "Show 'em whatcha got."

Angus made a slow turn and paused with his back to the crowd, feeling incredibly stupid.

"Fifteen hundred going once…" Charlie gave a long pause, "…going twice…"

"Five thousand dollars!"

Angus spun toward the sound of utter insanity, searching the faces for the one woman who'd shouted.

Every face in the crowd turned as well, and they all seemed to be looking at the lady standing beside Mona at the bar. The auburn-haired woman who'd, for a brief moment, reminded Angus of someone who'd stolen his heart so many years ago. His chest tightened, and he squinted against the stage lights, but couldn't quite make out her face.

"Sold!"

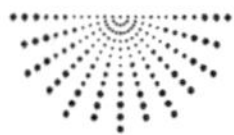

CHAPTER THREE

Gwen swayed, her hand held high, her lips tingling with the effects of the alcohol she'd consumed and the reverberation of the words she'd shouted at the top of her lungs.

Holy shit! What had she just done?

She'd spent five thousand dollars on a man. A man, for Pete's sake!

"Wow, Gwen." Mona laughed beside her. "When you decide to go all out, you go *all out*. I can't believe you just bought four dates with your old summer fling."

"I can't either," Gwen muttered, her heart racing at the thought of four dates with the man who'd never left her mind in the past seven years.

"I didn't even know he was on the lineup. He must have been a late add. Good for you." She clapped Gwen on the back, nearly knocking her over. "Congratulations!"

Staggering forward a step, Gwen struggled to stay

upright, with the room spinning and her stomach roiling.

"Are you okay, sweetie?" Mona leaned into her face. "You're looking a little green around the gills."

"I'm a little light-headed."

Fuck, fuck, fuck!

Gwen clapped a hand to her head. What had she done? Buying Angus was pure insanity.

"It's probably all that tequila making you dizzy," Mona concluded. "When was the last time you drank tequila shots?"

"Seven years ago." She hadn't had a shot of tequila since she'd been with Angus seven summers ago. *Holy hell. Holy hell.*

Gwen touched a hand to her cheek, marveling at how numb it was, kinda like when she went to the dentist for a filling and he shot her full of Novocain. Then she saw the look on Angus's face as he stared across the crowd of women, squinting. From his blank and confused expression, he hadn't recognized her.

"Holy hell," Gwen moaned. "What have I done?"

"You've just given five thousand dollars to the women's shelter." Mona's brows furrowed. "You do have five thousand to give, don't you?"

Gwen nodded. With each dip of her head, her vision swam and the murder of crows in her gut churned. "I've got the money, but why did I spend it on him?"

A grin spread across Mona's face. "Something tells me you're not quite over Mr. Angus McFarlan."

"I am. I really am. It's been seven years." Gwen threw her arm in the air and nearly fell over.

"There are some guys a girl never gets over." Mona slipped an arm around her waist and guided her toward the back door. "You need air."

"Air." Gwen's chest squeezed so hard she couldn't seem to breathe. "Yes, I need air."

"You're about to hyperventilate." Mona pushed through the crowd. "Out of the way. Give her some room."

As she was led through the crowd, women congratulated and thanked her for the sizeable donation.

"You lucky dog."

"Four dates. Wow! He's so hot he'd burn me."

"Wish I were in your shoes, or panties!" Mrs. Fenton said, her lips turning downward in a disappointed frown.

Gwen clutched her purse and staggered alongside Mona. When they made it to the door leading to the back of the building, Greta Sue appeared in front of them.

"Employees only in the rear," Greta said, her voice deep, her frown so fierce she scared Gwen.

Mona smiled at the big woman. "Oh, Greta Sue, you know me. I'm an employee on occasion. Let us go to the back."

Greta tipped her head toward Gwen. "She doesn't work here."

Gwen moaned and clutched her belly. The tequila, her purchase, the look on Angus's face were all working against her.

With a hand propped on her hip, Mona stared Greta Sue down. "Greta Sue, have a little respect for the woman who just contributed five thousand dollars to the women's shelter. Now either step aside, or find Audrey and we'll clear this right up."

Mona had more *cojones* than Gwen. The bouncer made Gwen shaky on her high heels.

Her frown deepening, Greta Sue shot a glance over her shoulder. "Audrey and Jackson are, er, busy in the storeroom."

Mona blinked. "Oh. Okay, then, just let us out the back door. Gwen is about to toss her cookies."

Greta Sue grimaced. "Why didn't you say so in the first place?" She stepped out of the doorway and waved them through. "The door will lock behind you. If you want back in, you'll have to come around the front."

"Will do." Mona hurried Gwen to the rear exit.

"Wait. I don't feel so good." Gwen stopped to lean against the wall and make the world quit spinning. It didn't help.

Mona bit her lip. "Maybe some ginger ale would help settle your stomach." She grabbed an empty cardboard box as she led Gwen out the back door. Before the door could shut, Mona stuffed the box in the gap.

The fresh night air should have helped, but it only cleared her mind enough to reinforce the crazy thing she'd just done. Gwen was committed to four dates with the man who'd broken her heart seven years ago. The stars in the wide-open Texas sky spun.

"Sit." Mona settled her onto a rickety, weathered picnic table beneath a scraggly live oak tree. "I'll be right back with some ginger ale. Don't go anywhere."

"I couldn't if I wanted to." Gwen laid her head on the

weathered wood, praying for the ground to open up and swallow her.

When Mona turned to leave, Gwen called out, "Wait."

Mona leaned close to her.

Gwen held her purse up without lifting her head. "My checkbook is in there. Get it out, write the check and I'll sign it."

"We can take care of that later."

"No. I don't know if I'll have a brain cell later." She shoved the purse at her friend. "Please. Do it, and deliver it to whoever's collecting."

"For the love of Mike." Mona dug out the checkbook and wrote the check. Then she placed the pen in Gwen's hand. "Your turn."

Gwen lifted her head only enough to see where to put her signature, scribbled her name and let her head fall back to the wood with a thump.

"You didn't even check to see if I put the right amount in."

"I don't care." Gwen closed her eyes. "I just want the world to quit spinning."

Mona swept a hand over her hair. "Oh, sweetie, you're wasted."

"No shit."

"I'll be right back." Mona left.

The music and the roar of the crowd from inside the building were muffled but still thrumming in Gwen's head, making her feel as though the world were rocking beneath her.

A mosquito buzzed around her ear, but Gwen couldn't lift her hand to swat.

Everything whirled. The stars, the sounds, the picnic bench, all around one central thought: she'd just bought herself a cowboy. Not just any cowboy. Angus McFarlan. A giggle rose up her throat and exploded in a bout of hysterical laughter.

Angus dropped down off the stage and tried to get through the crowd to the woman who'd placed the winning bid. But there was no pushing through the women. Their hands clutched at his naked chest, pulled at his arms and even tugged at the belt holding up his jeans.

Across the room, Mona had gripped the woman's arm and was leading her toward the back of the bar.

He had to get to her and buy back that bid. Four dates with a strange woman would be a nightmare. What would they have to talk about? Where would he be forced to take her? Fancy restaurants meant wearing a suit. Suits made him itch. Angus would almost rather go out with feral Old Lady Fenton than with the stiff-suited woman in the high heels.

When he reached the bar, he leaned over the counter. "Libby, where did Mona and that woman go?"

Libby's face broke out in a grin. "The winning bidder? Damn, Angus. I didn't know you had it in you. Five thousand dollars is a lot of money. You better treat her right."

His heart sank into his belly. Getting out of this mess

would be harder than he'd anticipated. Every woman in the saloon would remember this night because of the amount the woman had bid. No one had ever bid that much, as far as Angus knew.

Still, he had to try. Five thousand dollars. He had more than that in savings, but he needed it in case he had to come up with a down payment to buy the ranch from his mother.

The Rafter M couldn't leave the McFarlan family. He'd sell his soul to the devil before he let that happen. Not that the woman who'd bought him was the devil, nor was she the woman who would get his mother off his back.

He had horses to train and cattle to round up. Dating took time and a whole lot more effort than he was willing to put into it. And the woman in the suit had high maintenance written all over her beautiful body, right down to her pointed-toe stilettos.

Greta Sue was on the job, ushering the next poor slob up onto the stage to be auctioned off. With the bouncer out of the way, he ducked into the back of the saloon and threw open the first door he came to.

Stacks of boxes lined walls and shelves, while a barricade of cases of beer created another wall down the center of the little room. Plenty of liquor, but no Mona and no woman in a gray suit.

About to close the door and continue on, Angus heard a muffled giggle and a low groan.

"Mona?" he called out and stepped around the wall of beer cases.

"Oh, darlin', we've got company." Audrey Anderson

was seated on a short stack of boxes full of whiskey, wearing nothing but a bright-red bra, a pair of black, tasseled chaps and red cowboy boots, her legs wrapped around Jackson's bare waist. Her baby bump was as round as a cantaloupe and she was leaning back on her arms to give Jackson a better angle for what he was doing.

Jackson, shirtless and with his jeans down around his knees, glanced over his shoulder, his face tense. "Sorry, this storeroom's taken. And I'm having a helluva time finding a position that works. I'll be glad when the baby comes so we can go back to normal sex." He moved in and out of his wife, his knees bent, his angle awkward.

Audrey ignored her husband's surly grousing. "You're welcome to stay and watch, if you like. It makes me really hot when someone else is watching Jackson making love to me."

"If you stay, you have to promise not to laugh." Jackson sighed and pulled free of Audrey.

"Hey!" Audrey pouted. "I wasn't there yet."

"Honey, neither was I." He unlocked her legs from around his waist and lifted her off the boxes, setting her on her feet and kissing the tip of her nose. "I can't get the baby off my mind when we do a full frontal, babe. I'll have to come at you from the rear." He turned her around and patted her naked ass.

All the while, Angus stood there with his jaw slack and all his blood flowing south to his groin. He hadn't seen anything as incredibly hot as watching Jackson make love to his pregnant wife. "Uh, sorry. I didn't mean to interrupt." He backed a step, his cock hard. How long had it been since he'd been to the auction in Amarillo? He hadn't been in two months and damned if he wasn't feeling it.

Audrey bent forward, bracing her hands on the boxes in front of her. "I'm glad you stepped in when you did, Angus. I didn't think I could get any wetter, but you proved me wrong."

Jackson entered her from behind, sliding his damned big cock into her in one long, smooth glide that made Angus's mouth water.

"Yup, babe, you're definitely wetter. Damn, you feel good." He gripped her hips and pumped in and out of her. "But I'd like to think I'm the one making you wetter."

Angus frowned. "Won't you hurt the baby going so hard?"

Audrey laughed. "The baby seems to like it when Jackson rocks her to sleep." Her face tensed. "Yeah, now I'm feeling it. Faster."

"Going as fast as I can, sweetheart. You're a demanding little cuss."

"I know, I can be so bad," she said, her voice low and sexy.

Jackson slapped her ass.

Angus should have left the moment he spotted the couple doing it in the storeroom, but something about the wild abandon and happy coupling kept his boots rooted to the floor. But when Jackson slapped his wife's ass, Angus stepped forward and grabbed Jackson's arm.

"Hey, your wife's pregnant. You shouldn't be hitting her."

"Oh, Jackson, isn't he sweet? Angus is worried you're going to hurt me. You better not use the whip tonight." Audrey winked at the men standing over her naked ass. "For the record, Angus, Jackson never hurts me when he spanks me or uses the whip. But I might hurt him if he leaves me hanging here."

"Sorry, darlin'." Jackson started moving again, settling into a steady rhythm of pumping in and out of Audrey, his balls making a soft slapping sound against her skin.

"Yeah, now we're getting somewhere," Audrey moaned.

"The woman knows no shame, and she's been hornier than ever throughout this pregnancy," Jackson owned.

Angus closed his eyes to the lusty display in front of him. "I only came in here looking for Mona and the woman she was with tonight. They were headed back this way."

"Haven't seen them." Audrey's back arched and she sucked in a shaky breath. "I'm on the verge of coming. Angus, if you're going to stay, you have to play."

"Huh?" Angus stared at the woman. Had her pregnancy made her lose her mind? "Play?"

She plumped her full breasts. "Jackson's got that end occupied but you could make yourself useful and touch these."

Jackson growled. "Touch them, and I'm afraid I'll have to kill you."

"Oh, honey, you let your brothers touch me."

"We're married now. I don't mind someone else watching, but the girls are mine."

Audrey pouted. "Spoilsport."

His cheeks heating, Angus backed toward the door. "That's okay. I really need to find Mona."

"Try out back of the saloon," Audrey said, her attention shifting back to Jackson. "And you try what you just did again. Mmm…yeah…that."

His face burning all the way out to his ears, Angus hurried out the door and ran for the back exit. Never in his entire life had he walked in on someone else getting it on, not even his parents. He certainly didn't expect to be as aroused as he'd gotten. Embarrassed, yes. Aroused? Well, if he went by the tightness of his jeans, he was well on his way to another lonely night in a cold shower.

What killed him was that Jackson and Audrey hadn't been fazed in the least. Why was he so incredibly turned on by seeing them making love?

Two months without sex. That's why.

A box had been jammed into the door to keep it from shutting all the way. Angus kicked it aside and left the saloon, the door closing behind him.

For several seconds he stood beneath the yellow light shining over the back door, waiting for his eyesight to adjust to the darkness and his body to cool from overexposure to raw sex. Other than the muffled shouts and music from the Ugly Stick, nothing moved or made a sound in the darkness.

Until something that resembled a girlish giggle drew

his attention to the silhouette of a tree with a picnic table set up beneath it.

Another giggle erupted from the table.

"Mona?" Angus stepped off the back stoop and eased toward the picnic table.

"Mona, Mona, Mona. Wherefore art thou, Mona?" Another giggle and a woman's head rose from the table. "I can't believe I bought a cowboy." She giggled and hiccupped. "Damned tequila. Should be called to-kill-ya."

His vision finally adjusting to the starlight, he recognized the suit and sexy legs of the pretty woman who'd been the winning bidder.

"Oh good." Angus moved forward. "Ma'am, I wanted to talk to you about that bid."

"Angus, Angus, Angus. Where have you been for the past seven years?" She tipped her head so far back she swayed and would have fallen over had Angus not swooped in and caught her.

His heart lurched and his stomach bunched into an instant knot. "Gwen?"

"Oops." She giggled again, her hair slipping from the carefully constructed twist she'd had it in at the bar. Pins fell and the full, thick auburn hair he remembered so well slipped down around her shoulders and he fought back a sudden surge of joy. In the next second, a lead weight settled in his knotted gut, reminding him of why he shouldn't be happy.

Holy shit, this was the girl who'd ruined him for other women. The girl who'd made him fall in love with her one bright summer, only to leave him behind and never contact him again. He'd been nothing more than a summer fling. And here she was seven years later, having bought him in an auction. What kind of cruel trick was she playing?

"What's the matter? You look like you've seen a ghost." She leaned close to his face. "Boo." She kissed his mouth, her breath smelling of limes and tequila. Then she fell back against his arm. "Are you as wasted as I am?" Her head dropped back, her hair trailing over his arm, her body slack and her eyes closed.

"Damn it, woman, you better not pass out on me."

She lay as still as death, not a muscle twitching.

In that moment, Angus wondered if she'd drunk so much alcohol that she had alcohol poisoning. He laid his ear to her chest and listened for her heartbeat.

When he didn't hear it right away, his pulse kicked up and he shook her gently. "Gwen baby, wake up."

"Angus?" Her eyes blinked open and she smiled at him with the smile that had made his heart stop so many years ago. "When did you get here?"

"A few minutes ago."

"Good. You can take me to my room. I don't think I can drive." She yawned. "I'm too sleepy and my head is spinning."

"Just stay with me, will you?"

"Have to. Something's wrong with my muscles. I can't seem to move them." She raised her arm and let it fall around his shoulder. "See?"

Her head swiveled, her hair spreading across Angus's shoulder. The scent of honeysuckle wafted up, wrapped around his senses and made his knees weak with the rush of memories.

"Where's Mona?" he asked.

"She went to get me a drink," Gwen mumbled.

"You don't need another drink."

"Then take me to my room. I'm sleepy."

"Where are you staying?"

"I don't know. Somewhere in Temptation. A BBB." She giggled. "Why do they call them BBBs?"

"Bed-and-breakfast." Angus lifted her up into his arms.

Gwen dug her hands and face into his chest. "Whoa, stop the world. Let me off." She jerked her head up. "Wait a minute, I bought you."

Angus's arms tightened around her. "You bought four dates with me."

She poked a finger in his chest. "Damn right I did."

"I wanted to talk to you about that," he started.

"Nothin' to talk about. I bought you." She hiccupped. "'Scuse me. Damn, where was I? Oh yeah. Now you have to deliver." She poked him again and curled her fingers into the hairs on his chest.

"I want to buy back your bid."

She raised her hand, her fingers splayed. "Five grand. Holy shit, five grand. What was I thinkin'?" She stared into his eyes, her own blurred and glassy, and her face flushed. "Oh yeah. I wasn't thinkin'."

"Exactly. Let me buy back your bid," he begged, knowing this was a really bad idea.

"No, no, no." She shook her head side to side and shut her eyes tight. "Ooo, can't do that."

"What? Shake your head, or let me buy back your bid?"

"Both." She laid her cheek against his chest. "I need you, and I need for the world to quit spinning." Her voice faded and she went limp again.

"Damn." So much for talking her out of the dates.

"Angus?" A voice behind him made him turn around.

Mona stood with a paper cup in one hand. "I see you found Gwendolyn. Congratulations on bringing the highest bid in the cowboy auction's history."

"I'm sure they won't hold her to that bid. She was obviously stoned out of her mind."

"Not only is she going through with it, she's already delivered the check. The ladies from the women's shelter were ecstatic."

His heart sank into his stomach. Angus had no idea what Gwen had in mind when she bid on him. If she thought they would pick up where they'd left off, he wanted none of it.

Why had his mother meddled in his life? He was perfectly happy working the ranch, training horses and getting on with his life. Now he felt like his entire world had been flipped on its side.

"So what are you going to do about it?" Mona asked.

"I have no idea."

"Weren't you and Gwen a thing way back?"

His jaw tightened. "I don't know what you're talking about."

"Hmm." Mona nodded, her lips twisting. "You're gonna play it that way, huh?"

"Is she staying with you?"

"Nope. She's staying at that B and B on Main Street in Temptation, across the street from my shop."

"Then *you* take her there," Angus said.

Mona shook her head, a wicked grin tugging at the corners of her lips. "She won you fair and square. After she paid five thousand dollars for the pleasure of your company, I think it's only right you escort her home. Besides, she's in an upstairs room. I can't carry her."

Angus's eyes narrowed. "I can't leave the saloon. I'm designated driver for my brother."

"Colin?" Mona's smile turned smug. "He caught me on his way out. Molly O'Brien bought him on the auction block for a measly thousand dollars. She's giving him a ride home." She tipped her head. "Any more objections?"

His jaw tight, Angus bit down hard on his tongue to keep from saying something he would regret later. "Fine. Where are her keys?"

Mona set the cup she was holding on the picnic table and grabbed the purse on the bench where Gwen had been sitting. "She'll want her purse and I'm sure the keys are inside." She dug her hand in the bag and brought out an old-fashioned key with a room number engraved into it. "Here it is."

Mona laid the purse and key across Gwen's inert body. "Have a good night, Angus. Thanks again for volunteering to be one of our cowboys tonight."

"I didn't volunteer," he muttered.

Mona had already turned and walked away, chuckling as she went.

Hiking Gwen's limp body in his arms, Angus

marched around to the front of the building, to his truck. Once he had her settled in the passenger seat and buckled the seat belt around her, he rounded the truck and slid into the driver's seat.

When he'd rather be on his way home to have words with his mother for volunteering him to be auctioned off to the highest bidder, he was driving the opposite direction into Temptation to deliver a heavily inebriated woman to her room. A woman he'd spent the past seven years trying to forget.

She remained passed out for the drive into town and only moaned softly when he lifted her into his arms and carried her into the two-story colonial that had been converted into a bed-and-breakfast several years ago.

Once he had Gwen in the room, he carried her to the queen-sized bed and leaned over to lay her on the comforter.

"Mmm," she whispered, her voice gravelly and sexy as hell. "You smell good." With her hair down, her suit jacket open and several buttons on her light-pink blouse undone, she looked more like the girl he'd fallen in love with all those summers ago.

When he bent to lay her on the bed, she held on around his neck and wouldn't let go. It brought his face so near to hers it wouldn't take much to close the distance and kiss those full, rosy-pink lips.

"Stay with me," she said.

Images of Jackson making love to Audrey flashed through his mind, too fresh to dispel, and his cock hardened. He'd never made love to a woman as drunk as Gwen, and he had no intention of doing so now, even though his body burned with need.

"I can't," he said. "I have animals to feed in the morning." The reminder of all the work he had on his list for the next day should have brought him down. But when she stretched, her chest rising, her breasts straining against her soft pink blouse…

"For just a few minutes," she begged, her hands slipping up to cup the back of his head. She drew him closer until her lips brushed his.

Like a moth dragged to the flame, he couldn't break her hold, and for a long, delicious moment, he didn't want to. Too many nights he'd woken from dreams including her, only to find his bed empty, the sheets and pillow beside him cold.

He claimed her mouth, his tongue sliding in to stroke the length of hers, reveling in the taste and familiarity of Gwen. Her arms twined around his neck and she crushed her breasts to his chest.

God, she felt good. So good he wanted to strip naked and crawl into the bed beside her and make mad, passionate love to her through the night.

Angus froze. What was he thinking? The woman was drunk. He didn't take advantage of women who'd had too much to drink. It wasn't right.

When he straightened, her hands were locked behind his neck and she sat up, blinking. "The room is spinning." She giggled. "And it's hot in here." Gwen let go of him to shrug out of her jacket, getting tangled in the process.

Angus helped pull her arms free of the jacket and

slipped her shoes from her feet, his hands skimming across one shapely calf, electricity slicing through him, straight to his groin.

Damn.

"Still hot." She slipped the side zipper down on her skirt and shimmied out of it and the shirt. Finally flopping back against the mattress, patting the space beside her. "Stay."

Angus clenched his fists, fighting the urge to lie beside her, gather her close and feel her sweet skin against his.

Her pretty lips pouted and she stared up at him with a pleading look. "Stay until the room stops whirling." She smiled and closed her eyes, her breasts rising and falling with each breath.

When he turned to leave, she captured his hand and looked up at him again. "Please."

He glanced down into those hazel eyes that had exhibited every color of summer, and he knew he couldn't go. "Okay, but only for a minute." Calling himself every kind of fool imaginable, he lay on the bed beside her. For several minutes he allowed himself to stroke the hair out of her face and drag his thumb across her mouth. Her hair, her cheek, her lips were as soft as he remembered.

Angus snorted softly as he cupped her chin and pressed his lips to hers. Just one more taste. Gwen wouldn't remember it in the morning.

Oh, but he would.

What new kind of hell had his mother gotten him into?

CHAPTER FOUR

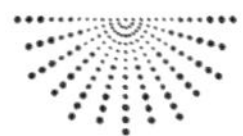

*I*ncessant banging crashed through Gwen's head. It jerked her awake and made her head throb. "I'm coming," she muttered, her voice gravelly, her mouth dry like someone had stuffed a wad of cotton in it.

When she sat up and opened her eyes, the sun stabbed her, slicing through her head, all the way to the base of her skull. It took a moment for her vision to adjust to the glare streaming through the window and to remember where she was. Ah yes, the bed-and-breakfast in Temptation. She couldn't remember how she got there. The last clear memory she could recall was sitting at the bar in the Ugly Stick Saloon and raising her paddle.

Her stomach roiled and she pressed a hand to it to keep from losing whatever was left in it.

More banging was followed by Mona shouting, "Gwen, wake up! I have Dalton with me."

Dalton. Oh dear Lord. Her son.

"Coming," she called out. Her words were barely above a whisper. Clearing her throat, she tried again, "Coming." This time the sound rang through her head and she winced.

One foot on the floor at a time. She stood and swayed, finally gaining her balance. That's when she noticed she wasn't wearing anything but her bra and panties. "Just a minute. I'm not decent."

Mona's chuckle echoed through the door. "I want all the details."

So did Gwen. She had no memory of undressing and her skirt and jacket were neatly folded over the chair beside her bed.

Grabbing the skirt and shirt she'd worn the night before, she pulled them on and buttoned the blouse. Wrinkled and smelling of alcohol, she hurried for the door, twisted the knob, yanked it open and was hit in the belly by the full force of an energetic little boy.

Despite the stabbing headache and her queasy stomach, she knelt to wrap her arms around the love of her life. "Hey, sweetie. Did you have fun spending the night with Uncle Grant?"

"Yes!" He hugged her tight and then stepped back. "We stayed up late, and made s'mores, and popped corn, and watched movies. It was the best! Can we do it again tonight?"

"I don't think so, baby. We don't want to wear out our welcome."

"Grant had as much fun as Dalton. I wouldn't be surprised if he starts bugging me to have kids." Mona winked. "I'd love to see a couple of little Grants running around the beauty shop."

"Or little Monas." Gwen straightened and winced. "Ouch." She pressed a hand to her temple. "Did I do what I think I did last night?"

"If you mean by getting totally shitfaced and blowing five thousand dollars on a cowboy, then yes." Mona grinned. "What I want to know is what happened when he brought you back here."

Heat rose up Gwen's neck into her cheeks and all the way out to her ears. She smoothed her hands over her son's ears and whispered, "You and me both."

Mona laughed out loud.

Gwen pinched the bridge of her nose. "It's not funny."

"I can't believe you drank as much as you did."

"I can't believe you let me bid on Angus."

"Honey, until you raised that paddle, I had no idea that was the way the wind was going to blow you." Mona crossed her arms "So, when's your first date?"

Dalton scurried off to find his favorite matchbox cars, leaving Gwen alone to stand up to Mona's scrutiny.

"There's not going to be a first date, or any date." Gwen glanced around the room. "I must have been really toasted. How did I get to my room last night? I don't remember walking up those stairs."

"You probably didn't. Angus must have carried you up them."

Gwen pressed a hand to her breast, her pulse still galloping. "Angus?"

"Yes. He brought you home because I told him there was no way I could get you up to your room when you passed out."

Gwen moaned and squeezed her eyes closed. "Will this nightmare never end?"

"I don't know. Angus is kind of dreamy. If I weren't completely crazy about Grant…"

Gwen opened her eyes and glared at Mona.

Mona held up her hands. "Don't worry. I have no plans to poach. Grant keeps me plenty happy." Mona glanced around the room, her brows rising at the twisted sheets. "You sure you don't remember anything from last night?"

Her shoulders sagging, Gwen scrubbed a hand over her face. Even her skin hurt. "Nothing."

Mona walked to the dresser and lifted a sheet of stationery. "Uh, sweetie, your cowboy left a message." She handed the paper to her, her lips twisting in an apparent effort not to grin. "Seems he's ready for that first date."

Gwen focused on the words written in a masculine scrawl across the page.

FIRST DATE. *Today at noon. Rafter M Ranch. Let me know if I need to come get you.*

SIGNED WITH A BOLD *A*, the message was clear, concise and completely insane. Gwen glanced at the clock on the nightstand. It was already eleven o'clock. That gave her exactly one hour to shower, take something for her splitting headache and get out to the ranch. "I can't do this."

"Oh, you can, and you will." Mona turned her around and aimed her for the bathroom. "You have just enough time to get ready. I'll stay and keep an eye on Dalton while you pull yourself together."

"It will take a lot more than an hour to pull myself together." She shoved the paper at Mona. "Call him and tell him I won't make him go through with this."

"No way. You said it yourself. Dalton needs a male role model. Angus is a good man, no matter that he dropped you like last week's garbage. He'd never hurt a kid." Mona put her hands behind her back, refusing to take the sheet. "Put your own insecurities aside and do it for Dalton."

Gwen pouted. "I'm not insecure. I'm the owner of a financially stable and growing business. You don't get that far if you're insecure."

"Yeah yeah blah blah. You've wasted three minutes arguing." Mona waved her hand. "Go." She gripped Gwen's arm, ushered her to the bathroom door and gave her a firm push to get her across the threshold. "I'll pick out your clothes." Her friend closed the door between them.

"I'm not going," Gwen said to door.

"Uh-huh. Shut up and get wet," Mona called out.

Grumbling, Gwen switched on the shower and stripped out of last night's clothes, wondering if Angus had taken advantage of her while she'd been out of it. She didn't feel any different. Her thighs weren't aching from making love and her pussy wasn't throbbing from a good fuck.

She shook her head, immediately regretting the movement. No, Angus wouldn't take advantage of a woman. His parents raised him to respect a woman's body. And boy, had he shown some real respect for her desires when he'd made love to her all those years ago. She should be glad he was such a gentleman, but part of her was disappointed. Maybe he wasn't even attracted to her anymore. Then again, Gwen wanted to be fully conscious and aware when they made love.

If they made love.

No no no.

Turning the temperature to cool, Gwen stepped beneath the shower's spray and let the water wash down over her heated skin.

Any idiotic idea of getting back together with Angus should be washed right out of her mind. She had a great life, just she and Dalton. It was full and complete the way it was.

Well, almost. Dalton did need a male role model so that he'd learn what it was to be a good man.

Ah hell. She had to go through with this, if only for the benefit of her son.

Angus might have dumped her all those years ago, but he was still a nice man and would be the right influence on her son. She could put up with four lousy dates. It would tide them over until her application for the mentoring program went through. Then she'd have another male figure for Dalton to bond with.

Hopefully, he would be interested in sports and the outdoors.

Ten minutes later, wearing a large towel, Gwen stepped out of the bathroom, her hair pulled back into a smooth ponytail. She'd applied just enough of her own makeup to conceal the dark shadows below her eyes. There was no disguising her bloodshot eyes, but a pair of sunglasses would serve the purpose.

"Here." Mona shoved a hanger at her. "You'll have to wear these. I can't believe you came to Temptation without a single pair of blue jeans."

When Mona had invited her to come down for a girls' night out, she hadn't thought much about what she was packing. She'd thrown in the first outfits she laid her hands on from her closet. Her nerves had been a little jumpy at the thought of going to Temptation. Mona always came up to Dallas to visit, knowing how Gwen felt about returning to the scene of her heartbreak.

Mona had been adamant that it was time for her to get out there and date again. Gwen would never have suspected she'd be going to the Ugly Stick Saloon for the Annual Cowboy Auction or that she would end up spending a sizeable chunk on her old flame. If she'd had any inkling, she might have brought a pair of jeans. Oh hell no, she wouldn't have. Gwen would have found some excuse to give her friend, on why she couldn't go to Temptation at all.

The only reason she'd agreed to go to the cowboy auction was that Mona had reassured her that it was ladies only, with no men but those on the auction block.

Having known how much Angus didn't like crowds and that wild horses couldn't have dragged him onstage to be auctioned off like one of his prized studs, Gwen felt relatively certain she wouldn't run into him.

Boy, had she been wrong.

Dressed in soft charcoal-gray slacks and a silk cotton blouse, Gwen stepped out of the bathroom, feeling more like the cool, calm, collected business owner, not the young college co-ed she'd been the last time she'd gone on a date with Angus. And this wouldn't be a real date. She'd have Dalton with her. With her son in the picture, she wouldn't be tempted to touch or kiss Angus.

Not that she would be tempted without Dalton in the picture. Angus was a chapter long closed in her life.

Dalton appeared in front of her, his eyes wide, eager. "Aunt Mona says we're going to a ranch with horses. Do I get to pet a horse? Can I ride one? Are they very big?"

Her head still throbbing, Gwen touched the top of her son's head. "Yes, we're going to a ranch, I don't know about petting or riding a horse. You'll have to ask the ranch owner about that. And yes, horses can be very big."

"I hope he lets us ride. Tyler has his own horse. Can I have a horse?"

"We don't have a place to keep a horse, Dalton."

"Then can I have a puppy?" Her son stared up at her, his big hazel eyes filling her heart. "You promised I could have a puppy."

"Yes, I did. When we move into a real house with a big fenced yard. Puppies need room to run and play."

"So do little boys," Mona reminded her.

Gwen frowned. "I know. I haven't had much time to house hunt lately, and what I've seen hasn't been right. I want it to be perfect."

"Sweetheart, no house is ever going to be perfect. You just have to find the one that's close enough."

"Yeah, I guess I am being too picky. Most of the homes in Dallas seem to look alike. I guess I want something like the little house I grew up in here in Temptation." She smiled, remembering the three-bedroom, white clapboard cottage with the wide front veranda and sage-green shutters hanging beside the windows. Her mother had planted flowers in the front garden and in pots on the porch, adding bright splashes of red geraniums, pink petunias and yellow lantana. Nothing said home like that little house with a big heart. She missed it and she missed her parents. Her eyes misted.

Mona patted her face. "Hey, you're going to a ranch, not a funeral."

"Did someone die, Mama?" Dalton asked.

"Oh my, look at the time." Gwen grabbed her purse and Dalton's hand. "We have to get going or we'll be late to the ranch."

Distracted from his question, Dalton raced for the door. "I want to ride a horse and pet a cow. Do you think they'll have puppies?"

Mona walked Gwen out to her car and held the door for Dalton as he crawled into the backseat and buckled his seat belt. "Be good for your mama and do everything she tells you." Mona leaned in and kissed Dalton's mop of dark-auburn hair. "Love ya, kid." She shut the door and looked over the top of the car at Gwen.

Gwen swallowed the lump in her throat. Mona had been there for her when her parents were killed in a car wreck. She'd been there in the hospital room when Dalton was born. Dragging her back to Temptation had all been an attempt to bring Gwen out of her shell and back into the world of mixing and mingling with people her own age. "Thanks for caring."

"Ah, honey. I love you and Dalton, and only want the best for you. Go have a good time on your date with Angus."

"For Dalton," Gwen said out loud, steeling her heart against more damage. At a good place in her life, she refused to put herself up for heartache all over again.

"Mom, you should have seen Angus's face when they called out his name as the next cowboy for auction." Colin laughed for the hundredth time that morning, riding on Angus's last nerve.

His humor had long since worn a hole in Angus's reserve of patience. Having been up since dawn, mucking stalls, feeding and exercising horses and taking care of the chores that had to be done before noon, he didn't have time or the desire to talk to the brother who'd deserted him at the Ugly Stick Saloon the night before.

"I'm sorry," his mother said. "When you boys put up such a fuss over my ultimatum, I guess I was a little angry. I didn't think Audrey would jump on the chance to add another two cowboys to the lineup on such short notice. But it'll all work out in the end." She smiled brightly.

"So you're not going to sell the ranch?" Angus asked.

Her smile slipped into a straight line. "I didn't say that. I meant every word I said yesterday. If you three don't get your lives together and make a go of finding someone to love, I'll sell this place and move to Florida. You two had better get crackin' because you have less than two months to make it happen."

Angus bit hard on his tongue. His mother had every right to do whatever the hell she wanted with the ranch. Legally, it was hers. "Fine. Since you put me up for bid and had me down for four dates, the least you could do is make lunch. My date will be here in…" Angus glanced at the clock, "…oh hell. She'll be here in fifteen minutes. I need a shower."

"I also meant what I said about not cooking or cleaning for you." His mother pivoted and left the room. She hadn't been kidding. That morning, she'd cooked eggs, bacon and grits for one, and made only a single cup of coffee in the coffeemaker.

Too frazzled, by his decision to go through with his dates, to cook, Angus made a very dissatisfying cup of coffee that tasted more like pond sludge and burned a piece of toast for his own breakfast.

His plan for Gwen's first date had been to take her on a picnic. He knew how to dress up and take a lady out to one of the high-class restaurants in Dallas, but he hated wearing a tie and hated more sitting for hours in a place he wouldn't feel comfortable. After seven long years, he'd be uncomfortable with Gwen anyway. He didn't have a clue how to start over with the woman he'd known so well, and he suspected he didn't begin to know the woman she'd become.

Now, he had to come up with something to feed his date. He was starting to rethink his picnic idea. "Damn."

Colin laughed out loud.

"You." Angus pointed at Colin. "I need two sandwiches pronto."

"What do I look like? Your maid?"

"I don't see you doing anything to save this ranch."

"I'm working on it."

"With Molly O'Brien?" their mother asked from the other room.

"Sorry, Mom," Colin called out. "Molly and I are just friends."

"Didn't she purchase four dates with you last night?" Angus asked.

Colin laughed. "Yeah, but like I said, we're just friends, and she needed a man to help her do some work on the little rental house she's refurbishing in town."

"I thought they were supposed to be dates," Angus grumbled.

"She told me what she needed, and promised to provide home-cooked meals if I provided the muscles." Colin grinned. "I've got four great meals in my near future."

"Right. In the meantime, make sandwiches." Angus snapped his fingers and pointed to the refrigerator. "And while you're at it, be thinking about how you're going to meet the woman of your dreams if Molly isn't the one. You heard Mom; we have less than two months."

Two months to find mates and to get their brother back in the state. Angus needed to have a talk with Colin about what went down between the two of them. Somehow they had to patch things up or they'd lose the ranch.

QUICKLY DUCKING INTO THE SHOWER, Angus washed the hay out of his hair and the manure out from beneath his fingernails. He got the feeling he could scrub all day and not measure up to the woman Gwen had become. When she was sober. She'd worn an expensive skirt suit, and those had been diamond earrings in her ears. Leaving him behind had been a good thing. Whatever she was doing with her life seemed to be working for her.

So why did she come back to Temptation? And why did she purchase four dates with him? Seven years was a long time.

Whatever reason she had, Angus didn't care. He refused to get any more involved than the four dates he was obligated for. No touching, holding hands or kissing.

Hell, last night should not have happened. He should have taken her to her room, dumped her on the bed and left immediately. Instead, he'd stuck around and kissed Gwen like there weren't seven years since the last time. Now all he could think about was how soft her lips still were, the scent of honeysuckle in her hair and the way her breasts pressed against her shirt with each breath she took.

He'd stayed with her to make sure she didn't get out of bed and stumble outside and down the steps. After she'd fallen into a deep sleep, he'd lain longer, drinking in the vision of the woman she'd become, all soft curves, long legs and toned muscles.

He turned the shower water to cold and stood beneath the spray until he shivered and all desire had been effectively chilled. It was self-defeating to think of making love to Gwen. She'd left him seven years ago without so much as a goodbye kiss or note. No forwarding address and no phone number.

Hoping she'd call him when she got to College Station, he'd waited by the phone every evening, praying for it to ring. It hadn't. His plan to go to look at a horse in the college town where she'd gone to school had fallen through when his mother was diagnosed with breast cancer. His entire life went on hold then.

All of Angus's focus went to caring for the ranch and his mother during and after her surgery. He'd gone with her for every round of chemotherapy, as determined as she was to beat the illness. He couldn't stand to lose another one of his parents so soon after the first. Theirs had been a tight, loving relationship.

Almost a year passed when he finally felt his mother was stable enough to leave without worrying himself or her. He'd gone to the college town where Gwen went to school, hoping to find her, only to discover he'd missed her graduation by a week. She'd moved out of her apartment and hadn't left a forwarding address with her landlord. The fact she hadn't left a forwarding address or phone number told Angus she was cutting all ties. She wasn't interested in being found.

His heart aching, Angus went home and got on with the rest of his life just fine without Gwen in it.

Angus stepped out of the shower, dried off with a big, fluffy towel and strode across the hallway to the bedroom that had been his since he was born. He had only left the ranch when he'd gone to college and for the three years he'd worked in Dallas at a high-powered architectural firm. He still worked for the firm on a contracting basis, having set up office in his father's old study. Angus had modernized the room with a computer, high-speed satellite Internet and his drafting table standing in one corner. Though he'd given up a chance at the major projects and advancing in his career, he still used his skills, added value to the corporation and kept up with changes in the field.

If he and his brothers didn't live up to his mother's demands, he'd have to move all of his things. Maybe even go back to Dallas and work full time for the corporation where he might be another warm body in a cubicle. Or he might earn a chance at eventually leading one of the major projects. Though, his desire to scratch his way to the top had been trumped by his desire to work with the animals on the ranch.

And what would he do with the horses? He'd built a profitable horse breeding and training facility he didn't want to give up. It was one of the purest pleasures he got out of life. Working with the horses calmed him and reminded him what was important in life. He understood the horses and they seemed to have an equal understanding of him.

Some of his clients called him the horse whisperer. He laughed at the moniker. Anyone could work with horses if they had the patience. Angus felt more comfortable with the big animals than he did with people. They didn't squander his love, they returned it. He liked working as an architect, but he was more passionate about working with the horses.

Pulling on a clean pair of jeans and a blue chambray shirt, he ran his fingers through his damp hair and jammed his feet into his boots. The sound of tires crunching on gravel made his heart beat faster and he turned to stare out the open window.

A sleek champagne-colored Cadillac pulled up the drive.

This was it. Once again he considered talking her into selling back her bid, but he needed to save every cent he had to purchase even a portion of his family ranch. He might ask to take on additional contracts at the corporation in Dallas. Unfortunately, it wouldn't give him the funds fast enough. Perhaps he'd be better off taking on a full-time job with a respected company to encourage the bank to lend him the money needed to purchase the property or a portion of it.

The horses were his, purchased with the money he'd earned through his architectural contracting and his quarter horse breeding program. But finding a place he could keep all thirty animals wouldn't be easy on short notice. If the ranch sold fast, he might have to sell all or part of his herd.

Cinching his belt buckle, he left his room and strode out to the porch.

"She's punctual." Colin leaned against the porch railing, his gaze on the car pulling to a stop in front of the house.

"Sandwiches?" Angus asked.

"I made two."

"Out of what?"

"Are you seriously going to get picky?"

Angus frowned, his gut clenching. "Just answer."

Colin shrugged. "The usual. Bread, lettuce, tomato, mustard."

"And?"

With a cringe, Colin's gaze slid to the corner of the porch. "We're going to need to make a grocery run to town."

"What else is in the sandwiches?"

"The only lunch meat in the refrigerator was a package of bologna."

"Damn it."

Colin glared at him. "I did the best I could with what we had."

The car door opened. Realizing in that second that it was too late to slip into town for groceries, Angus grit his teeth and prayed this date would end as soon as it started.

He couldn't be that lucky.

A long, slim leg encased in charcoal-gray trousers swung out. Another followed and Gwen stepped out of the vehicle, her hair pulled back in an artful twist, displaying the long, slender neck Angus had loved kissing. She wore four-inch high heels and large, round sunglasses on her pale face.

After closing her door, she turned to the rear door of the vehicle.

Angus squinted, wondering what she was doing.

Then two little legs dressed in pint-sized blue jeans appeared below the edge of the car door. When Gwen closed the back car door, a little boy stood beside her with a shock of thick auburn curls and a grin the size of Texas.

Angus couldn't mistake the kid for anyone else's. The little boy looked so much like Gwen it hit him like a punch to the gut.

Colin laughed. "Holy crap. She's got a kid."

Angus didn't see anything funny.

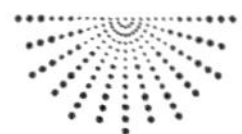

CHAPTER FIVE

Gwen stood for a moment, her gaze catching his, her teeth worrying her bottom lip. It was too late to change her mind. Either her plan worked, or it didn't. She held her son's hand in hers and marched up to the porch.

"I'm here for my date," she announced.

"Looks like I'm gonna be makin' another sandwich." A man who had to be Angus's brother punched Angus in the arm as he went by. "Mom will be ecstatic when she sees this."

The front screen door opened and a woman Gwen recognized as Angus's mother stepped out. She looked much the same as the last time she'd seen her seven years ago. A few more gray hairs, but the same bright eyes and welcoming smile. "Boys, don't be rude, invite your guests inside." She walked down the steps, beaming at Gwen and the little boy. "Since my sons seem to have forgotten their manners, I'm Maggie McFarlan. And you are?"

Disappointment tugged at Gwen's heart. It wasn't as if she'd spent that much time around Angus's mother seven years ago, but it would have felt good to be remembered. But it was Angus and Gwen's fault Mrs. McFarlan didn't remember. They had been more interested in spending time alone and often naked. "Hi, I'm Gwendolyn Graves."

Angus's mother's brows dipped into a V and she tapped her chin. "Gwendolyn." She stared hard at Gwen. "I know you, don't I? I never forget a face."

Gwen's lips formed the hint of a smile. "You used to make chocolate chip cookies when I came to the house."

The older woman's eyes rounded. "Gwen? The woman who broke my Ang—"

"Mom!" Angus stepped in and cupped Gwen's elbow. "Perhaps we can take Gwen and her little boy inside for some lemonade."

His mother's brows rose. "Do we have any made?"

Angus's brother rolled his eyes. "Of course not, but I could make some darned good coffee."

Gwen smiled. "It's too hot for coffee, but a glass of water would be nice." Anything to redirect Mrs. McFarlan's frown from her.

"Water it is. But first…" Maggie McFarlan's frown lifted and she bent down to Dalton, "…who do we have here? I don't believe we've been properly introduced."

"This is Dalton, my son," Gwen offered.

Mrs. McFarlan hugged the boy. "Well, now, aren't you a handsome man?"

"Yes, ma'am," Dalton said.

Gwen hid her smile.

Mrs. McFarlan straightened, her face softening as she stared down at the boy. "He looks just like you."

Gwen nodded. "He looks a lot like the pictures of my father when he was a boy."

Angus squatted in front of Dalton and held out his hand. "I'm Angus. How do you do?"

Her son studied Angus as if he was sizing him up. Finally he placed his little hand in Angus's big one. "I'm fine, thank you."

"That's a mighty strong grip you have there." Angus stared into the boy's face and asked, "How old are you, Dalton?"

"I'm five and a half. I'll be six on my next birthday." He held up both hands and showed an awkward array of six fingers.

As Angus straightened, Gwen gave him a narrowed glance, a spike of anger rushing into her chest. "He's not yours, if you're wondering." Dalton hadn't been conceived until nearly a year after Gwen left Temptation.

"Hey, big guy. I'm Angus's brother Colin. Come give me one of those big handshakes." Colin sat on the porch steps and held out his hand.

The boy glanced from his mother to Colin.

With a smile, Gwen said, "It's okay."

The boy crossed to Colin and held out his hand.

Angus leaned toward Gwen. "Why didn't you tell me you were married?"

Gwen's chin tipped up and she stared at him down the length of her perky nose. "It wasn't important."

Angus gripped her arm and forced her to take several steps backward to get her out of earshot of his mother, who had joined Colin on the porch steps, talking with Dalton. "The hell it isn't. We kissed."

She planted her fists on her hips. "It doesn't count since I didn't know what the hell I was doing."

"Obviously."

"Hey. Don't judge me." Her chin tilted up another notch. "You don't know anything about me."

"I used to," he gritted out.

"Past tense." She sighed, the tension easing a little from her body. "For the record, I'm not married."

"Then how do you explain your son?"

"I don't have to explain anything to you." She had been married for one month and a day. The marriage had only been intact that long due to paperwork and court dates. "I'm here for a date. Are we going on one or not?"

Angus's gaze slipped to Dalton who was engulfed in one of his mother's bear hugs. "What about the boy's father?" He glanced back at Gwen.

Her lips twitched. "He's not coming on the date."

His mouth pressing into a tight line, Angus gripped her arm. "That's not what I was asking, and you know it."

Gwen rolled her eyes. "I know, but I find I like yanking your chain." Her gaze went to her son. "His father has never been in the picture." She'd sent word to him, via certified mail, a few days after she'd had

Dalton, but hadn't heard from him since the night they'd conceived the boy. Gwen preferred it that way. At least Dalton wasn't torn between two homes with legally mandated visitation.

"What do you expect to do with him while we're on our date?" Angus asked.

Gwen bit her bottom lip. "He's coming with us." She held her breath and waited for Angus's response.

For a long moment, he didn't say anything, just stared from her to Dalton and back to her.

"Are you using him as some kind of shield? Because if you are, there's absolutely no need. I won't kiss you again."

She was going to tell him the same, but his beating her to it left her feeling a bit hollow inside. Which was silly. With no claim on the man and no desire to rekindle their old relationship, she was there for Dalton. Nothing else.

"The reason I bid on you last night wasn't for me. You see, I need a man." Her cheeks burned and she hurried to explain. "I'm a single mother, and I love my son dearly, but I can't provide everything he needs in the way of guidance and life lessons. Last night I was discussing our needs with Mona. She suggested I enroll Dalton in the mentoring program."

"Angus, we're going inside to raid my secret cookie stash." Mrs. McFarlan took one of Dalton's hands and Colin took the other.

"Wait. You have a cookie stash?" Colin asked as they entered the house.

Gwen edged toward the house. "Maybe we should

go along with your mother. This is a new environment for Dalton."

"He'll be fine." Angus stepped in front of Gwen. "Go on with your story. I'm curious to know how I fit in this picture."

"Well…" She wet her lips and fought for the right words, when she knew what she had to say didn't sound as good as it had the night before when she'd been three shots of tequila deep into fixing all her problems. "I bid on you as a jump start for Dalton. From what I remember of you, you'll make a fine role model for my son. Four dates with you will give him a good idea of what it takes to be a man and will tide him over until I can get him enrolled in the mentoring program and find him a suitable mentor." She cringed and waited for the tirade.

Angus seemed to chew on her revelation for a while before talking. "Let me get this straight. You paid five thousand dollars for me to be a role model to your little boy for four dates?"

When he put it like that, it sounded a little crazy.

Gwen nodded. "Yes."

"That's a lot of money for playdates with your son."

"It was for a good cause. I probably would have donated that much for the women's shelter anyway."

Angus was already shaking his head. "No deal."

Gwen's eyes narrowed and her belly clenched. "What do you mean?"

"I mean, you bid on four dates with me. Not with me and your son."

"What's it matter if it's just you and me, or you, me and Dalton?"

"The definition of a date is two people spending time together. Nowhere in there is a child part of that equation."

Anger pushed steel into Gwen's spine. Dalton was as much a part of her as the lungs she used to breathe. She lifted her chin. "That's the way I want to collect on my bid."

Angus crossed his arms and stood with his legs slightly apart. "Look, I get your reasoning, but it changes everything in the terms of this agreement. If you want me to play role model for four dates, that's a whole different ball of wax than four dates one-on-one. I propose this—"

Gwen held up a hand. "You can't just change the rules."

"Sweetheart, you did when you brought your son into the picture."

She didn't have a comeback. He was right. Her next step would be to free him of his obligation.

But, damn it, she didn't want to! "You still owe me four dates," she said stubbornly.

"Here's the proposal I was going to suggest before I was interrupted." He raised four fingers. "I'll give you four role-model playdates with you and your son, if…" he paused, drawing out her last nerve to the breaking point.

"If what?" she demanded.

"If we follow through with the dates as originally agreed upon at the auction."

"Huh?" Gwen's eyes narrowed. "Isn't that what I suggested in the first place?"

"No." His mouth curved upward. "I'll spend four days with you and your son. And you'll spend four nights with me on dates—without Dalton."

"What?" The air rushed from Gwen's lungs and refused to return for several long seconds. "You want to date me? I have a hazy memory of you trying to buy back my bid last night. Why the turnaround?"

"Ah, so your memory is returning." He flashed a wicked smile.

That smile cost her another round of hyperventilation. Seven years ago, he'd smiled his way right into her panties. And she'd been glad to let him in. The man was so damned sexy and his casual modesty had been as endearing as his looks.

"You want the equivalent of eight dates with me?"

With a nod, he repeated, "Four with you and Dalton to teach him man things and four just you and me."

"What would we do on those dates?" Her eyes narrowed. "And you can leave kissing and sex out of the mix."

Angus spread his arms wide, his hands palms up. "Did I say anything about sex and kissing? I won't ask anything of you that you don't want to give willingly."

"Good, because I have no intention of getting involved with you again."

A brief shadow crossed his face. "Good," he echoed. "I don't have time for such nonsense."

"Then why extend the obligation out to eight?"

"Let's just say I need a break. If I'm committed to

going out with someone, I can't work through and skip it."

She stared at him long and hard, noting the fine lines around his eyes and the dark smudges beneath them. If anything, they made him look even more rugged and handsome than he did seven years ago. He'd aged well. But eight dates? Gwen wasn't sure she could stand up to that many and not make herself insane with longing.

She was beginning to think this entire ordeal was a bad idea. As a single mother, she didn't want to drag her son into a relationship that would leave him heartbroken. Would four visits with Angus break Dalton's heart?

Gwen chewed her lip. Parenting was hard enough, without having to guess what would hurt her son. This man had hurt her once. She wasn't so sure she could handle it again. Could Dalton?

"We can start today with the first of the playdates with Dalton and tonight we can get one of the real dates over with."

"Over with." Gwen snorted. "You make it sound like torture."

He shrugged. "It is what it is."

"This is new for you."

"What?"

"Being vague." Gwen ran her gaze over him. "The Angus I knew was always direct. He didn't waste words."

"Because that Angus wanted to get right down to making love."

His smoldering gaze made Gwen's blood heat and a slow burn build at her core.

Angus's face smoothed into indifference. "Since sex is out of the picture, no need to be direct." He stuck out his hand. "So, is it a deal?"

Again Gwen's eyes narrowed. "I still don't buy why you want eight dates instead of four, but sure. It's a deal." She gripped his hand and regretted it immediately.

Electricity shot up her arm and spread through her body like a wildfire in a Texas wind. She jerked her hand back as if it had been singed. "And I meant it. No sex or kissing."

Angus raised his hands. "I'm not even suggesting it. If you want to be kissed, you'll have to ask me."

"Don't worry. It'll never happen." She turned and strode toward the house.

"Never say never, sweetheart," Angus said behind her.

"And I'm not your sweetheart," Gwen retorted. *Not anymore. You had your chance seven years ago.*

ANGUS FOLLOWED Gwen into the house, enjoying the view from behind. Her hips were a little rounder and she had her hair pulled up in another one of those darned twists that hid the auburn curls he used to love getting lost in.

Why he'd come up with that "deal" he didn't know. Her adamancy about not getting involved with him again grated. He suspected that was the reason he'd come up with the cockamamie plan. Anything to prolong her torture. Unfortunately it meant he'd have to endure it as well.

What did he know about little kids, other than what he'd learned helping to raise his younger brothers? They were family and his mother and father had done most of the parental guidance. He'd helped Brody and Colin when they were learning to ride horses, although it had all been kind of natural. They'd grown up around the animals and knew no fear of them.

"Does Dalton know anything about what goes on at a ranch?" Angus asked.

"Nothing."

"What about sports?"

"I enrolled him in tennis lessons, but they haven't begun. And he's been playing soccer since he was four." She smiled. "He's actually pretty good at it for his age group. Some of the kids stand in the grass and pick flowers. Not Dalton. He goes for the ball and gets it down the field."

The love and pride were clearly evident in Gwen's gaze and tone.

Regret tugged at Angus's gut. If Gwen hadn't gone back to college after that summer, or if he'd been free to go after her, Dalton might have been his little boy.

"What about riding?" Angus held the front door open for her. "Has he ever been on a horse?"

She shook her head. "No."

With a nod, he followed her into the house. His picnic idea just got more difficult, but not impossible.

He found his family in the kitchen. Dalton stood on a box by the counter, helping Colin.

"I'm making a peanut butter and jelly sandwich." Dalton turned and showed Gwen his hands smeared with peanut butter and grape-colored goo. "We're going on a picnic and riding horses."

Gwen smiled at her son. "That's nice." Her brows rose as she turned to Angus. "I'd have brought jeans with me had I known."

"Don't worry," Colin said. "I'm sure Mom will have some you can wear."

Angus's mother eyed Gwen. "Of course I do, but they'll probably be too big and too short."

"They'll do for riding," Angus said. "She can cinch them with a belt." As well-dressed as Gwen was, he figured it would make her nuts to wear someone else's ill-fitting clothes. All the better. Putting her off her game would make him feel better, more in control of a situation that could get out of control all too quickly.

Gwen raised her hands. "I don't have to go. You and Dalton might enjoy a picnic without me."

"Oh no, you should definitely go. Angus will enjoy a day off working so hard. And I know Dalton would prefer to have his mother along with him in a new place," Angus's mother said. "I'll be right back with something that will work just fine." She hurried out of the room before Gwen could protest further.

Angus didn't like how his mother had gone from almost spilling the beans about Gwen breaking his heart, to practically welcoming her and her son into the family. And he didn't like how quickly she'd taken to the little boy. Maybe agreeing to eight dates was a mistake. If his mother got attached to Dalton and Gwen, she'd be disappointed when the dates were over and everything went back to the way it was before the auction.

"Really, I don't have to go," Gwen said.

"Colin went to a lot of trouble to whip up sandwiches for us. I would hate to disappoint him," Angus said.

Colin wiped off Dalton's hands and helped him down from the box. "You wouldn't disappoint me at all. In fact, I would gladly stay here and entertain Gwen while you and Dalton go for a ride." He hooked Gwen's arm in his. "Why is it Mom and Angus know you, but I don't?"

Angus's teeth ground together and he fought the urge to knock Colin's arm off. "You were backpacking across Europe that summer after you graduated from Texas Tech." He'd had to come home early when their mother was diagnosed. "Gwen, as you heard, this is my brother Colin."

"I'd have skipped Europe to have a summer with you, Gwen." Colin winked across at her and shot a teasing glance at Angus. "Stay here with me."

"Colin, behave yourself. She's going with Angus." Angus's mother entered the room carrying jeans, a blue chambray shirt, belt, socks and a pair of cowboy boots. "I didn't have a shirt that would fit you right, so I got one of Angus's and the boots belonged to Colin when he was a teen. They were too fancy for him so he never wore them and I never got around to donating them to charity. If they fit, you can have them."

"Thanks." Gwen took the armful of clothing, and

Angus's mother led her down the hallway to a bathroom.

"I didn't realize the woman who bought you was an old flame." Colin chuckled. "That makes this situation even more interesting."

"She's not old and she's not a flame." Angus stared at the little boy who looked so much like his mother. "I guess what you're wearing will do for a ride."

"Do I get to ride a horse all by myself?" Dalton stared up at Angus, his eyes wide and so much like his mother's Angus found himself automatically liking the kid.

Angus shook his head. "Not this time. For today, we'll let the horses get used to having a small boy around them, and you can get used to how big they are."

"I'm not afraid." Dalton's chin lifted just like his mother's when she faced a challenge.

Angus couldn't help but smile, and he ruffled the boy's hair. "I bet you're not. But the horses might be afraid of a little person wandering around them. You have to promise to do exactly as I say."

He pressed one hand to his chest and raised the other. "I promise."

"Then we'll get started while your mother is dressing."

Colin handed him a woven Mexican blanket and the canvas bag with the sandwiches. "Enjoy. Mom is over the moon."

Angus glared at his brother. "She better not get too used to it. This means nothing."

"Actually, you better hope it does mean something. For the sake of keeping the ranch."

"You're on the hook too," Angus reminded his brother. "When are you going to kiss and make up with Brody?"

"That day will never happen."

"Then today is a waste of effort."

Colin sighed. "*You* have to contact Brody. He hasn't talked to *me* in years."

"What did you two fight about?"

Colin shrugged. "Something that never should have happened."

His mouth twisting, Angus nodded. "A woman."

"Not much gets by you, brother. Not much." Colin clapped him on the back. "Good luck. That one will be really hard to resist. And frankly, I don't know why you would."

"Says the man who can't resist a single woman," Angus muttered, heading for the back door. "At least I can restrain myself."

"Yeah. I can see that." Colin's laughter followed Angus and Dalton across the kitchen.

With Dalton at his side, Gwen dressing somewhere in the house, Angus hoped he wasn't setting himself up for a big fall.

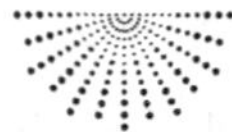

CHAPTER SIX

Angus opened the back door and waited while the boy stepped out. As they walked down the steps, Dalton slipped his little hand into Angus's and smiled up at him, his eyes sparkling with excitement.

Angus's chest tightened. He could get used to having a little guy like this around. The child found joy in just being there, and Angus found that joy to be more than a little infectious.

Five minutes later, Angus had the gentlest mare on the ranch tied to a post inside the barn and a saddle thrown over her back. Dalton stood at the mare's nose, smoothing his hand over her muzzle, watching every move and asking questions as Angus cinched the girth. He was eager and smart as a whip. Like his mother.

"You two starting without me?" Gwen's warm voice melted over Angus like hot butter on a roasted potato.

"Mama, this is Fancy. Isn't she pretty?" Dalton called out, standing perfectly still as he'd been told.

Angus finished cinching the girth and let the stirrup fall into place before he turned to Gwen.

She wore the jeans his mother had loaned her tucked into the borrowed cowboy boots. The waistband was pulled tight with a belt around her narrow waist. But it was the blue chambray shirt tied at the waist, exposing a little skin at her midriff that gave Angus's heart palpitations.

Gwen had rearranged her hair into a French braid at the back of her head. She looked so much like the college coed Angus had fallen in love with that the years rolled back and he almost pulled her into his arms and kissed her like he would have if it had been seven years ago.

But it wasn't.

"Watch Dalton while I saddle another horse, will ya?" he said, his voice gruffer than he'd intended. This whole ordeal was going to be harder than he'd thought. How was he going to get through eight dates when he was having trouble with the first one with the kid?

Angus left the barn and walked out into the heat, welcoming the distance from Gwen. He needed a minute or two to get his shit together before he went back in the barn. For once Joe, the bay gelding he would ride that day, didn't play Keep-Away. He came right up to Angus and nuzzled his chest as if sensing the human's unrest.

Angus snapped the lead on his halter. "At least you don't have girl troubles."

The horse snorted.

"You're right. Neither did I until last night. But what can I do?"

Joe gave him a gentle shove toward the barn.

"Okay, okay." Angus smoothed a hand over the gelding's nose. "If I didn't know better, I'd swear you were working with my mother on this matchmaking thing. Well, just get it out of your mind. I'm not interested in long term."

Joe tossed his head and whickered, the sound more like laughter than Angus cared to admit.

The horse seemed to know more about the future than he did.

Leading Joe, Angus returned to the barn and tied him up to the post next to the mare.

Gwen ran her hand across the sorrel's neck. "Fancy's beautiful. Is she one of the horses in your breeding program?"

He nodded. "She was my prime breeding mare until I retired her last year."

"Will Dalton be riding with me?" Gwen asked. "It's been years since I got on a horse."

"You'll have no problem picking it up again." He remembered how natural she'd been when he'd taught her to ride. Her body moved with the animal's rhythm. "But, no, the boy will ride with me."

Once he had Joe saddled, Angus helped Gwen up on Fancy and then lifted Dalton onto Joe's saddle. "Hang on to the horn."

Placing his boot in the stirrup, Angus swung up into the saddle behind Dalton. The boy's face split into a huge grin and stayed lit up the entire ride out across the pastures to the swimming hole where Angus had planned to have a private picnic, just he and Gwen.

Dalton was full of questions about the ranch, cattle, hay, snakes, coyotes and the clouds above. By the time they pulled the horses to a stop, Angus's ears were sore from listening and he'd talked more than he normally talked for an entire month.

He swung down from the saddle and held up his arms for Dalton, who leaned out, trusting Angus to see him safely to the ground.

Once his boots hit dirt, the boy darted for the creek and the pool of water where Angus and Gwen had skinny-dipped on more than one occasion.

Gwen's gaze rested on her son and the water beyond, her cheeks a pretty pink. Angus guessed she remembered too. Were her memories as clear and erotic as his?

He doubted it.

Taking Fancy's and Joe's reins, he tied them to saplings on the creek's edge where they could get a drink of the cool, clear water. Then Angus rummaged in the saddlebag for the blanket and spread it out in the shade by the pool. He went back to the saddlebag for the sandwiches and bottled water.

Gwen glanced his way and nodded. "Dalton, it's time to eat that sandwich you helped make."

"Oh boy!" Dalton skipped to the blanket and sat cross-legged. Within minutes he'd gobbled down half of the sandwich, drunk some of the water and yawned.

Gwen patted the blanket beside her. "Lie down."

"I'm not sleepy," Dalton said and yawned again.

"Then lie down anyway and stare up at the clouds." Gwen lay down beside him. "See that one?" she pointed. "It's shaped like a boat."

"I see it." Dalton glanced at Angus. "Aren't you going to lie down too?"

Angus smiled at the two, his heart swelling at the picture they made. If he wasn't careful, he'd fall right into that trap and wish he were a permanent part of that picture. When Dalton looked at him with those eager eyes, he couldn't say no. He stretched out beside Dalton and stared up at the clouds. "I see a giraffe."

He remembered playing that game with Gwen when they'd lain naked in the warm sun, drying off after a swim. Only the game never lasted long because they ended up making love and falling to sleep in each other's arms.

After a few minutes of cloud gazing, Dalton's eyes drifted shut and his breathing deepened.

Gwen lay for a few minutes more, then she rose and stretched her arms over her head, the movement raising the shirt up her torso, exposing more of her creamy, smooth skin.

Angus swallowed a groan, stood and checked on the horses.

When he turned around, Gwen had moved down the hill to the edge of the creek and sat on a rocky ledge, her boots beside her, her toes trailing in the water.

Angus fought his urge to go sit beside her and lost.

He passed the blanket where Dalton slept curled on his side, his cheeks flushed, a smile playing at his lips, probably dreaming about riding his own pony.

Angus stood next to Gwen for a long moment, staring at the water below with a yearning he hadn't experienced in a very long time.

"We had fun that summer, didn't we?" she said softly.

He didn't respond.

"What happened?" she looked up at him.

"You left."

"I had to go back to school."

He frowned. School was important and he didn't begrudge her return, but he still felt the hurt of her leaving without saying a word. "You could have said goodbye."

She turned, her brows furrowed. "I couldn't do it without breaking down. I said it all in the letter and gave you my phone number and the address of my apartment."

"What letter?"

"I slipped it into the back pocket of your jeans the last night we were together. We were here." She waved her hand at the copse of trees, the creek and the pool. "You fell asleep before I did. I put the letter in your pocket for you to find later, after I'd gone." Her eyes widened. "You didn't get it?"

He shook his head. "No."

"But it was in your jeans right where you'd find it."

Those jeans probably went right into the wash. The letter would have disintegrated.

"As far as I knew, you slipped away in the night without so much as a kiss."

"I had to go. I wouldn't have left if you'd told me to stay." She smiled, though her eyes were awash with unshed tears. "I guessed it wasn't meant to be. When I hadn't heard from you in weeks, I figured you weren't all that in to me."

Oh, but he had been. Everywhere he'd turned had reminded him of her. The ranch became a nightmare of reminders.

When his mother was diagnosed with cancer, he'd given up any thoughts of returning to Dallas and a fast track in his career, to contract as an architect from home on the ranch, giving him the latitude to gear up for the fight of his mother's life. His father's death was the reason he'd been home that summer he'd met Gwen. His mother's diagnosis had been his reason for staying.

"I guess it doesn't matter now." Gwen shrugged. "We were young. I'm a mother now, and I have to be focused on what's good for Dalton."

Angus sat beside her and tossed a rock into the water, disturbing the mirrorlike surface. The ripples spread out, diminishing the farther away they were from the point of contact. "What about what's good for you?"

She sighed. "I can wait. Dalton needs me."

"And you don't need anyone?"

Gwen picked up a rock and tossed it into the water. "No."

When she reached for another rock, Angus captured her hand. "If I'd known about the letter…"

"Would it have made a difference?"

"Probably not. My mother was diagnosed with cancer. After my father's passing earlier that year I couldn't leave. Things got a little crazy."

"I'm happy your mother survived." She sat with her hands clasped together in her lap, her lips pressed together, her eyes glassy with unshed tears. One escaped the corner of her eye and trickled down her cheek, landing on her hand.

She stared down at the hand. "It's all water under the bridge, right?" Slipping her hand out of his, she stood. Her hair had loosened on the ride and a strand curled around her cheek.

Angus rose and reached out to brush it back behind her ear like he had so many times before.

Gwen's eyes widened and she stepped back quickly. "Don't—" She didn't get to finish her sentence because she'd stepped back too far and her heel came down on the curved edge of the stone ledge. Her body swayed backward, she flung out her hands and tilted toward the water.

Angus grabbed her hand and yanked her back from the edge, crushing her in his arms.

For a long moment Gwen rested her hands on his chest, her breath short and labored.

Angus's heart beat hard against his ribs, his hands splayed across her back. He didn't move, didn't breathe for fear of spooking her, like a timid colt. If he stayed still, she wouldn't remember that she didn't want to be kissed and he could sneak in and…

Gwen tilted her head up, her hazel eyes smoky, her tongue slipping across her lips.

If she hadn't done that, Angus was almost certain he could have resisted. But when that tongue slipped over her lips, his focus zeroed in and he had to taste them.

He lowered his head, but at the last minute remembered his promise not to kiss her unless she asked for it. Hovering over her mouth, he prayed for a miracle.

"Please," she whispered.

That's all it took and his lips connected with hers, his tongue pushing past her teeth to caress hers in a long, slow glide. He savored the flavor of her mouth, all minty and fresh, sexy, hot and moist. It wasn't enough. He slid his mouth lower, blazing a path over her jaw.

When she tilted her head back, exposing the long, slender line of her neck, he took that as an invitation to go lower, nibbling her with his lips, tonguing her skin down to the pulse beating wildly at the base of her throat.

She circled her hands around his waist and down to cup his ass.

Sweet Jesus.

He remembered the way her cool fingers felt running across his naked skin, making him want to shed every piece of clothing and tear hers from her.

Running his hands up under her shirt, he nearly wept when he realized she wasn't wearing a bra. His fingers found a distended nipple and he squeezed it, flicking it until it tightened into a hard bud. He stepped closer, nudging her thighs apart, his cock straining against the denim of his jeans.

The summer just got hotter and if he wasn't careful he might burst into flame.

"We shouldn't," Gwen whispered against his ear, her hands saying the opposite as they slipped into the waistband of his jeans and slid down over his buttocks.

"You're not making a good case for stopping," he said, nibbling on her collarbone, his thumbs circling her nipples.

Her chest rose and fell on a sigh. "We have to. Dalton will wake up soon."

The horses nickered as if to agree.

Gwen jerked away from him and shot a glance at her son sleeping on the blanket. Then she turned away from him and stared at the water. "I remember the first time we went skinny-dipping here." Her voice was little more than a whisper.

"So do I. I was shocked."

She snorted. "You were so hot and horny I could practically smell the pheromones. If I hadn't taken the first step and stripped naked, it wouldn't have been long before you did it for me."

His pulse pushed molten hot blood through his veins, his groin throbbing in remembrance. Angus stood behind Gwen and wrapped his arms around her waist, his hands splaying across her bare midriff. "Tell me to back off, and I will."

"What about Dalton?"

"I can see him, but he won't be able to see us if he wakes."

Instead of pushing him away, she slid one of his hands inside the waistband of her jeans and down to the triangle of silk covering her mons.

Drawing in a ragged breath, Angus slipped his fingers beneath the wedge of fabric and curled his fingers into the tuft of silky curls.

Gwen's breath caught on a gasp and she cupped his hand, urging him closer.

Taking her lead, he slid his finger between her folds and tapped the tip of her clit.

Her back arched into him and her head pressed against his chest. "I'm on freakin' fire," she moaned.

"Babe, that's only the beginning." His finger edged lower, dipping into her warm, wonderfully wet entrance and swirled. Then he returned to that strip of nerves he knew was her pleasure center. If she hadn't changed in the past seven years, he knew if he made her happy there, she'd come apart.

Starting out slow, he alternated between stroking her clit and dipping into her juices, teasing her entrance. His cock grew as hard as concrete, pressing into her buttocks.

With Dalton sleeping up the hill behind them, Angus didn't attempt to satisfy his own urges, but he could certainly satisfy Gwen's. The faster he flicked and swirled, the more Gwen's hips moved, undulating to the rhythm he set. Her breathing grew more ragged and her body tensed.

With a short, jerky movement, she grasped his other hand and shoved it beneath her shirt, giving him free rein over her breasts.

He pinched a nipple and thumbed the peaked tip.

"Oh man," Gwen whispered, her voice strained, her hands cupping his, urging him to go faster, squeeze harder, dip deeper. He gave her one, then two, then three fingers, finger fucking her until she squirmed.

Then her body went rigid and she stilled his hands with hers. "Wait."

For a long moment, she stood as still as a statue, then her entire body shook with the force of her release, and the breath she'd been holding came out in a long, sexy moan. "Holy shit, Angus, that was incredible."

He held her, one hand cupping her sex, the other squeezing a breast, basking in her afterglow, wishing he could lift her and settle her over his aching dick.

When she finally sucked in a deep breath and let it out, Angus lifted his head and glanced toward the blanket where Dalton was just sitting up, rubbing his eyes. "Um, party's over." He reluctantly removed his hands from her body.

Gwen stepped out of Angus's arms, straightened her shirt and jeans and then hurried over to her son. "Hey, sleepyhead. Did you have a good nap?" If her voice was husky, Dalton didn't notice.

But Angus did and his chest swelled. He walked to the creek and rinsed his hands in the cool water, tempted to submerge up to his waist to chill the hard-on pushing against his denim fly.

After several calming minutes, he turned back to the mother and son.

Gwen sat on the blanket, with Dalton on her lap, smoothing a hand through his hair. "Are you ready to head back?"

"No," Dalton said, blinking in the sunshine. "I want to ride all day."

"We can't take up all of Mr. McFarlan's time. He has chores to do."

"I want to help with the chores. I'm strong." Dalton lifted his arm and bunched his muscle. "See?"

Angus chuckled. "He *is* strong. But your mother's right. We need to get back to the ranch. I have to feed these horses and a dozen others."

Dalton pouted, but got up and helped his mother fold the blanket.

On the ride back, the boy leaned back against Angus, his body relaxed. "I like riding horses. Can we do this again?"

"You bet." The boy's trust in him and eager anticipation of another day together filled Angus with warmth he'd never experienced.

Dalton twisted in Angus's lap to stare up at him. "Tomorrow?"

Angus smiled down at him. "It's up to your mother."

"We have to get back to Dallas so that I can get ready for work on Monday."

"When can we come again?" he asked.

Angus stared over at Gwen. "Next Saturday?"

"Can we, Mama? Can we? Please?" Dalton gripped the saddle horn, excited but not so much so that he'd lose his seat.

Angus kept a firm hand around the boy's middle to steady him.

"If it fits with Mr. McFarlan's plans."

"Does it?" Dalton stared up at Angus, his gaze wide and hopeful.

"Sure." They'd reached the barnyard by then and Angus glanced across at Gwen. "Are you headed back to Dallas tonight?"

She shook her head. "I have the room at the bed-and-breakfast until the morning. I'd planned on staying one more night."

"Then I'll pick you up at eight o'clock." Angus swung his leg over and dropped to the ground, reaching up to lift Dalton out of the saddle.

The little boy wrapped his arms around Angus's neck and hugged him. "Thank you for taking me on my very first picnic."

Angus's heart skipped several beats. "Your first?" He looked over the boy's head at Gwen.

She nodded. "We don't get many opportunities to have picnics in Dallas."

Angus set the boy on the ground and reached up for her.

Gwen let him grip her around the waist and lift her out of the saddle. But he didn't set her on the ground right away. He let her slide down his body, his arms circling her. "Tonight?"

Her eyes flared and her cheeks flushed. "I don't know."

"What's wrong?" He held her, refusing to let go. He liked that he was making the sophisticated Gwen nervous and confused. "Are you afraid?"

Her clear hazel gaze met his and she said, "Yes. I am. We can't just pick up where we left off. Things aren't the same. *I'm* not the same."

"You didn't answer." He leaned in as if to kiss her, his mouth hovering over her lips, refusing to touch them. "Yes or no?"

"I don't have a sitter."

"I'll ask my mother. She loves kids. Especially boys."

She inhaled, her chest rising against his. She released the breath and said, "I'll think about it. If I agree, I think we need to go back to the original plan: no kissing or sex."

"I promise not to do anything you don't want me to."

Her eyes narrowed. "You've already broken that promise."

He grinned. "No I didn't. If I recall, you asked me to kiss you. You even said please. I didn't do anything you didn't want me to do." Setting her away, he gathered the horses' reins and Dalton's hand. "Come on, you can help me and your mama brush Fancy."

"Really? I get to brush Fancy?" He trotted alongside Angus to keep up.

As they removed the saddles and groomed the horses, Angus couldn't get over the domestic picture they made. He, Gwen and Dalton.

He regretted that they'd lost the past seven years. But regret wouldn't bring them back. If he'd found that note in his back pocket, his life might have turned out a lot differently. If his mother hadn't had cancer, he'd have gone after Gwen sooner. Now that he'd found her, and he'd learned that she hadn't just walked out of his life, he wondered if there could be a future for them. It might take some convincing, but just maybe.

GWEN'S PULSE wouldn't slow, and she couldn't think straight the entire time she spent brushing the horse and keeping Dalton from walking behind the mare's backside and getting kicked. Every time she glanced up at Angus, she could feel the intensity of his gaze, and heat shot straight through to her aching, throbbing core.

By the time they were finished with the horses, her insides were so hot she wouldn't have been surprised if she spontaneously combusted and burned the barn down. In the space of five minutes with Angus's hands in her pants, she'd had the most intense orgasm she'd had in seven years. And, Lord help her, she wanted more.

Several times she had to remind herself to breathe so that she wouldn't hyperventilate and pass out at the hooves of the mare. Dalton would be traumatized, wondering if she'd died or been hurt. How would she explain she was having heart palpitations from the aftereffects of being stroked by the tips of an orgasm-inspiring set of fingers?

As they walked back to the house, Gwen held Dalton's hand. Dalton angled toward Angus and grabbed the big cowboy's hand in his free one.

Her heart hurt. They looked so much like a family. But she couldn't let herself believe that fairy tales really did come true. If she spent too much time with Angus, she risked falling for him all over again. And if things didn't work out, it wouldn't be just her getting hurt this time. She refused to let Dalton be the collateral damage of her lousy love life.

"Tonight," Angus said as they climbed the porch steps.

"Tonight?" Mrs. McFarlan sat in the porch swing

sipping a glass of iced tea. "Come sit with me, sweetie." She patted the empty space next to her.

Dalton ran to the swing and climbed into the seat beside Angus's mother.

The sight of him and the older woman together brought a lump to Gwen's throat. Her parents had died in an auto accident three months before Dalton was born. He'd never know his grandparents and his father's parents weren't alive either. Gwen had looked them up only to discover they'd died before she'd even met Dalton's father.

"Are you two going out tonight?" Mrs. McFarlan asked, her face open and all smiles.

"I don't know," Gwen stalled. Going out alone with Angus had heartache written all over it. "Maybe not tonight—"

"We will, if we can find a sitter for Dalton," Angus said. "I don't suppose you know someone who might be interested?"

"Dalton can stay with me," his mother announced. "We can play horseshoes until dark or play cards until your mama comes back. What do you think, Dalton?"

"Can I, Mama? Please?" Dalton sat beside Mrs. McFarlan, perfectly at home with the woman. Gwen had been banking on the fact that Mona and Grant had another commitment and wouldn't be able to watch Dalton while Gwen and Angus went out on the agreed-upon date. That would have given her time to tamp down her rising desire for the man. After the earth-shattering orgasm by the creek, she was still shaking with the amount of effort it had taken to force herself to break free of his embrace and pull herself together when Dalton woke. Physically breaking away hadn't been so hard because Angus hadn't been holding on too tight. He'd let go immediately.

Gwen hadn't wanted to let go.

No no no.

She couldn't do this. It was supposed to be all about Dalton. A night alone with Angus could prove disastrous.

"In fact," Angus's mother went on, "how would you like to stay the night on the ranch? You could build a tent in the living room out of old blankets and furniture."

"Really? A tent in the house?" Dalton looked at Gwen. "I'm going to build a tent in the house." He jumped out of the swing and grabbed Mrs. McFarlan's hand, tugging hard to get her out of her seat.

"Now? I meant later. After the dinner Colin is going to fix." She started for the door. "Oh well. I guess I could gather the blankets." Pausing beside Gwen, she asked, "If it's all right with you."

Gwen raised her hands, feeling as if decisions were really being taken out of her hands and everything was moving too darned fast. "I wouldn't dream of spoiling his fun. Yes."

Dalton ran into the house, shouting at the top of his lungs. "Yay! Uncle Colin, we're going to build a tent."

Uncle Colin? Gwen's heart tugged once again. Dalton didn't have a single uncle or aunt. For the past six years since her parents' deaths, it had only been Gwen and Dalton. She'd struggled to take care of him, taking off work when he was sick, shifting her schedule to make it to his sporting events and being there for him as much as possible. She was his mother, father and all the family he had. But she couldn't be everybody, and she missed having an extended family. Dalton had so much love in his heart; he needed more people to love and be loved by. Perhaps she was depriving him by not remarrying and giving him and herself the extended family they both needed.

Gwen turned to Angus. "Okay. I guess I'll see you at eight." She entered the house, changed into her own clothing and would have left the jeans and shirt in the bathroom, but as she opened the door Mrs. McFarlan walked by with a stack of blankets.

"Oh, honey, keep those old clothes. Who knows where Angus will take you on a date. He can be so unconventional. It wouldn't hurt to have a spare."

Gwen left the house with the old jeans, a pair of slightly large cowboy boots and the shirt that smelled so much like Angus. She'd never be able to get rid of it. Likely she'd hug it every night before she went to sleep, wishing things had been different.

She had no idea how she'd make it through the evening without hugging the real thing. Damn it, if she wanted to maintain her sanity, she had to.

Who was she kidding? She didn't have to be a psychic to see how doomed that plan was to failure.

CHAPTER SEVEN

Angus and Colin worked silently as they fed the animals, mucked the stalls and turned the horses out to pasture.

"Well, how did your family date go?" Colin asked on the way back to the house. "Did having a kid along cramp the Angus McFarlan style?"

Angus shot his brother the finger, having no intention of telling him what had transpired between him and Gwen. Hell, he was still struggling to keep from hardening every time he thought about how completely Gwen had given herself to him. "Have you called Brody to apologize and ask him to come home?"

"What's that got to do with your date?" Colin grumbled.

"Nothing. I just want to know what you're doing to fix what's broken between you and Brody."

"*You* talk to him."

"I'm not the one who pissed him off enough he'd

stay away from home for eight years. You better get on it or the two months Mom gave us will be over before you even find him."

"Fine. I'll call him tonight."

"Call him *now*."

"Don't push me."

Angus ground to a halt. "I sure as hell will if you don't get off your high horse and call him."

"You don't have to bite my head off."

"Then grow some testicles and apologize. Family is all we have, and we haven't been acting like much of one lately."

Colin's lips slipped upward in a smirk. "You're sounding more like Mom than yourself."

"Well, maybe it's time I wasn't myself." Angus walked away feeling more conflicted than ever.

"Not yourself?" Colin chuckled. "Does it have anything to do with one hot chick who rocks a tight, gray skirt?"

"It has to do with me." Angus stopped, sucked in a deep, steadying breath and went on, "My life has been on hold for far too long."

"On hold? You've been working your ass off making this ranch work, and look at all you've accomplished. A sustainable business and the best quarter horse breeding program in the country."

"At what cost? It's like Mom said, who would I leave it to? What's the use of building up a great legacy if you don't have a family to pass it on to?"

Colin's eyes widened. "Wow, Mom really got to you, didn't she? And Gwen. And how good she made baggy jeans and an old shirt look… Yeah. I can see she rocked your world. But I'm not ready to settle down. The way I see it, I'm three years behind you on the power grid. That's three more years of living and loving every female I can get my hands on. Why settle for one?"

"You're wasting time. We have two months before Mom sells the place. I don't plan on being homeless when I've put too damned much time and effort into this place. And I want my children to know where they came from and have a place to call home."

"Okay, okay." Colin blew out a breath. "I'll call Brody."

Already riled and anxious about his date that night, he didn't have time for all the drama that had dragged on far too long between his brothers. Angus blasted through the door and didn't slow down until he hit the shower. His mother was right. The three of them had needed a swift kick in the pants to make them grow up and see that life was passing them by.

Angus hadn't asked for it, and had convinced himself he didn't want it, but he'd gotten a second chance at the woman he'd fallen in love with so long ago. He'd be damned if he squandered it this time around. He'd also be damned if he let his brothers' rift be the reason his mother sold the family ranch.

At fifteen minutes after seven o'clock, Angus was dressed in his best blue jeans, boots and a crisply ironed, white, button-down, long-sleeved shirt. He'd dusted off his best cowboy hat and polished the belt buckle he'd earned during the one year he'd ridden broncs on the rodeo circuit. As he passed the living room, he heard childish giggles coming from under a half-dozen blankets strung across the living room. The sound warmed his heart.

"Dalton?" he called out.

The little boy's auburn head appeared from beneath the draped edge of a blanket. "Sir?"

Angus squatted down next to him and peered into the tent city. "This is some setup you have here."

"Uncle Colin helped me build it. Wanna come in?"

"Maybe later. Where is Uncle Colin?"

"He's getting a shower and Memaw is making hot dogs for us."

"Memaw, is it?" She'd gone on a cooking strike for her own sons, but she'd feed a stranger's son. Angus smiled. Figures. The woman had a big heart, especially where children were concerned. And little boys had always been her favorite. Angus wondered how she'd react if she had a granddaughter. He wondered himself how he'd like having a little girl trailing around behind him in the barn. "Hey, Dalton, what kind of flowers does your mama like?"

The boy shrugged. "I don't know."

"How about what *color* of flowers does she like?"

He smiled and announced, "White."

"White?" What woman liked plain white flowers?

"Whenever she gets them from the store, she lets me pull the petals off until the last one."

"You pull off the petals?"

"Yes, sir. The white flowers with the yellow in the middle." He ducked back into the blanket fort.

Colin appeared barefoot in a clean T-shirt and jeans. "Did you decide to stay and play in the fort with us?"

"No." Angus straightened. "I'm leaving now."

"Go get 'em, tiger." Colin slapped his back a little harder than was necessary.

"Hey, what kind of flower is white with yellow in the middle?" Angus asked.

"White with yellow in the middle?" Colin gave him a blank stare.

"The kind you can pull petals off," Dalton said from beneath the blankets.

Colin grinned. "Daisies."

With the answer he needed, Angus headed for the phone in the hallway and dialed Bunny Leigh, the owner of Temptation's only flower shop.

"Sweet Temptations, this is Bunny."

"Bunny, it's Angus. I need flowers," he said without preamble.

"Now? The shop closed two hours ago."

"I know. But I'll pay double if you can get me a dozen daisies."

"Double?" Bunny cleared her throat. "Is your mother in the hospital? You tell Mrs. McFarlan I'll be by tomorrow to visit."

"No. My mother is perfectly fine."

"Then why the emergency flowers?" Bunny gasped. "Wait. Didn't you go to the highest bidder last night? And wasn't she your old flame?"

News traveled fast in a small town. Gritting his teeth, Angus bit out, "Can you get me the flowers or not?"

"Hey, you're cranky. Is it because you're not getting any and you hope to by giving her daisies? I'm telling you. Sex bribes come better in full, lush, fuck-me red roses. I can set you up with two dozen, just say the word."

"I don't want roses, and they aren't sex bribes. I want a dozen very sincere daisies. If you don't have them, just say so."

"Oh, I have them."

"Holy hell, Bunny, stop teasing me, already." Angus took a steadying breath. "Will you sell them to me tonight?"

"Sure. What time do you need them and do you want them delivered?"

"I'll pick them up in fifteen minutes."

"You don't give a girl much time to think about it, do you?"

"That's the idea," he muttered as he ended the call.

"MONA, what am I going to do?" Gwen had called an emergency meeting with her old school chum and only confidante. "I can't go out with him."

"Why not? You paid for him." Mona's eyes narrowed. "Or is it because you don't trust him?"

"Hell no. I trust *him*. It's *me* I don't trust!" Gwen paced the small bed-and-breakfast room in nothing but her bra and panties. "Besides, I don't have anything to wear!" She threw her hands in the air and paced faster.

"Hey, hey." Mona stood in front of her and grabbed

her shoulders. "Snap out of it. You could probably wear nothing at all and suit him just fine."

"I know!" Tears sprang from Gwen's eyes. "Damn. I swore I'd never cry over that man again."

"And all these years you thought he didn't care about you. He'd never gotten your note and he thought you'd run out on him without so much as a goodbye."

"Exactly. Now you see why my life is so fucked up. I can't afford to let go of the old hurt. It was the only thing holding me together."

Mona pulled her into a tight hug. "Oh, baby. You can't hold on to that hurt. It was groundless."

"I have the worst luck with men."

"Two men. One due to a misunderstanding. The other due to a mindless mistake in Vegas. You were young, depressed and looking for love in all the wrong places."

"Damn right I was."

"I remember. I found Grant at a rodeo. It wasn't Vegas, but a girl can do some pretty stupid things at a rodeo. Things didn't work out for us at first."

"But everything worked out fine in the end between you and Grant. Why can't everything work out fine for me?"

"It can if you let it."

"No. I won't subject Dalton to the heartache. If he gets used to having Angus around, he'll be devastated when we break up and he doesn't come around anymore. And if it works out between Angus and me, how can I expect him to take in another man's child? It's hard enough to be a parent to your own children, much less someone else's."

"Honey, Dalton is the sweetest little boy in the world. Angus will love him. Especially since he's the spittin' image of the woman he loves."

"He doesn't love me." How could he when he'd thought she'd dumped him without a word all those years ago? God, what a waste. "Hell, it's been seven years. He's probably had at least that many lovers since me."

"That cowboy wouldn't have expanded the dates if he didn't have feelings for you." Mona shook her. "Woman, he freakin' doubled them! That says something."

"I'm so confused." Gwen shoved a hand through her heavy mass of hair. "I'll never be ready in time. Hell, I haven't even done my hair."

"All you really need to do is brush it and leave it down. When you wear it up, you look older than you are." Mona hugged her. "No offense, but you look uptight."

"I *am* getting older, and my hair is completely unmanageable when I don't put it up."

"Wear it down," Mona commanded.

Gwen popped a salute at her friend. "Yes, ma'am."

"Tell you what, I have a dress you might be able to wear." Mona spun and sprinted for the door. "I'll be right back."

"Why don't I come with you?"

Mona laughed. "You'd be arrested for indecent exposure. You get yourself a cup of tea while I run across the street. I'll be back in three shakes."

After Mona left, Gwen's panic levels rose exponentially. Without someone to talk her down off the ceiling, she clung to the rafters. Making herself sit in one of the two easy chairs in the room, she pulled her wallet out of her purse and dug a photograph out of a hidden pocket.

The picture was of her and Angus that summer when she was only twenty-one and he was twenty-five. Mona had taken it of them kissing. They looked so in love it brought tears to Gwen's eyes. "I can't do this."

"Yes, you can," Mona said from the door, breathing hard. "And I have the perfect dress for you to wear."

"What if he takes me four-wheelin' on the flats out by the lake?"

"Then you hang on tight." Mona patted her arm. "Don't worry, Angus is seven years older than the last time you dated. He's not going to take you mud ridin' or four-wheelin'. My bet is he'll take you somewhere the two of you can stare at the moon or each other, whichever melts your butter. Then he's going to turn that horse-whisperin' magic on you and charm you right out of your panties." Mona held up an accordion of condom packets. "That's what these are for."

"Mona! There will not be sex tonight." Though she protested, her loins ached at the very thought. Hell, he'd given her a breath-stealing orgasm with Dalton nearby. "Fuck! Now you've got me thinking about it."

"That's right." Mona grinned. "You'll be in a full lather by the time he arrives."

"I already am," Gwen wailed. "I'm trying to come down from it. Holy shit. I can't handle this much stress."

"Sweetie, you're not handling this reunion very well. Take a deep breath and let it out ."

Gwen sucked in a shaky breath and let it out slowly. "I don't feel any better."

"Well *I* do. That was a whole two seconds you weren't freakin' out on me." Mona shoved the dress into her arms. "Now, go try on this dress. It's a surefire way to get laid tonight. I guarantee it."

"What part of *I don't want to get laid* did you not understand?"

"Blah, blah, blah. You're not foolin' me, even if you *are* foolin' yourself." Mona unzipped the back of the dress and held it up for Gwen to slip into.

Gwen had to shimmy into the formfitting dress that hugged her body like a second skin. The front neckline plunged halfway to her belly button, displaying a lot more boobage than she'd shown in public since she was two and playing in her wading pool in the nude. The back plunged so low she suspected her butt crack showed.

"Lose the bra," Mona said.

Gwen unhooked her bra in the back and slid the straps from her shoulders, then slipped her arms into the dress. "I can't wear this. It screams *fuck me*, all over the place. And look at this." She plumped her breasts. "The girls are barely covered."

A knock on the door made Gwen jump. She glanced at the clock and nearly had a cow. "Shit, he's early." She adjusted the bodice of the dress to cover as much as possible, marched to the door and yanked it open. "You said eight o'clock—" Her words lodged in her throat at the sight of the gorgeous cowboy carrying an embarrassingly large bouquet of daisies.

"I was in town early so I thought I'd see if you were ready." He glanced behind him. "I can come back in fifteen minutes."

"No. No." She stepped aside. "Come in."

"These are for you." He held out the flowers. Her favorites.

When she took them, the shock of electricity blasted through her all over again. It had been that way seven years ago, and the same held true today. The man made her insides melt and butterflies war in her stomach. What was it about Angus McFarlan that turned her world upside down with just one of his smiles? It was going to be a lot harder than she originally anticipated to walk away from the man this time. Of that she was certain.

But damned if she could do it now.

"Ahem." Mona cleared her throat. "I'll just be going." She stepped around them to slide through the doorway. "Angus, treat my girl right. And I don't mean all gentlemanly and the like. Treat her right." She winked at Angus, and then turned to Gwen. "Call me when you get a chance. I want all the details. That's right," she whispered to Angus. "We share everything." She waved her fingers. "Toodles."

With Mona gone, Gwen had nothing standing in the way of her and Angus. Her nerves tightened and she dove for the strappy stilettos Mona had brought with the dress. "If I'm overdressed, I can change into the jeans your mother loaned me."

His gaze swept the length of her, from her hair tumbling about her shoulders, down the dress's plunging neckline to the tips of her bare feet. "You look great."

Her cheeks heated at his compliment. "Where are we going?"

"I thought I'd take you to dinner at the steak house and then back to the Ugly Stick Saloon. If I recall, you like to dance."

"I do." She smiled up at him. "And if I remember correctly, I taught you how to two-step."

"You had the broken toes to prove it."

She wiggled her toes, remembering, and feeling more relaxed than she had before he'd arrived. "Well, then, let's get going. I'm hungry." If they kept it light and kept to public places, she might make it through the night without pouncing his body and begging him to fuck her like there was no tomorrow.

ACCORDING TO PLAN, they ate at the steak house, talking over dinner about the people they both knew from Temptation and about the changes that had occurred over the past seven years to the town and the Ugly Stick Saloon.

Gwen had a single glass of wine, determined not to overdo it after having tied one on the previous night. Not knowing what would happen between the two of them after their four dates, she wanted to savor every moment.

"What about you?" Angus asked. "How did you come to own your own business at such a young age?"

"Seems I have a knack for knowing which products will take off and which won't. It was a small company with a limited budget and marketing plan." Gwen smiled. "The owner was in her late sixties and ready to retire. She wanted to sell the company to someone who had vision and could take it to the next level."

Angus nodded. "You were her choice."

"That was the beginning. I had to come up with the business plan and financing to buy it. With her help and a lawyer friend of mine, we made it happen. Three years and thirty additional employees later, I've increased sales three hundred percent and we're moving for the second time to a larger building."

"You seem very happy."

Gwen shrugged. "It's been a challenge to get the right people in the right positions. I finally feel I can take a vacation and not worry that things aren't being run the way I would if I were there twenty-four-seven." She leaned back, twirling her wineglass in her fingers. "What about you? Are you still contracting with the engineering firm in Dallas?"

He nodded. "I am."

"I don't know how you have time, with a full-scale quarter horse breeding operation and cattle ranch."

"I have two full-time ranch hands who help keep me sane, and who take over when I'm on deadline or have to make a trip to the firm in Dallas. But I'm not managing nearly as many people as you are."

"You're managing a large number of animals and acreage, which has its own headaches."

His lips curled in a half smile. "Having worked in Dallas in a large engineering firm, I find that I'm much happier working with horses."

Gwen laughed. "I think it suits you much better. You always had a way with them."

"And you always had a way with people."

Her chest swelled. Since her parents had died before she purchased the company, she really had no one with whom to share her triumphs.

"You should be proud of your success, Gwen."

"Thank you. And so should you."

He shrugged. "I do what I do because I love it."

"Same here. I figure if you don't love what you're doing, you're not doing the right thing." Gwen's heart warmed. She blamed it on the wine, but suspected it was more the company. As they finished eating, the warmth morphed into something more. In her mind, she imagined several different scenarios, all of them more graphic than the last, each including some form of undress and bodily contact.

By the time their table was cleared and Angus held her chair, Gwen's pulse was hopping and her nerves had stretched to a hypersensitive level that had her nearly panting in anticipation.

Angus offered her his arm.

Gwen nearly sizzled with the jolt of electricity that passed from where she touched him, through to her very core. Though he was being the ultimate gentleman, Gwen reacted as if he were stroking her body with the tips of his fingers and his tongue. Her pussy creamed and thrummed with a pulsing need she could no longer deny. She'd been foolish to set the ground rules of no kissing and no sex, when she was ready to throw in the towel, admit defeat and get naked.

"We don't have to go to the Ugly Stick if you don't want to," she offered, praying he wouldn't think she'd rather end the night there. Other more intimate ideas plagued her mind to the point of obsession.

"Good. I'd rather not share you."

Gwen slowly released the breath she didn't realize she'd been holding and smiled at his comment. It sounded promising.

"I have a better place in mind." Angus held open the door to his truck.

"You do?" God, she hoped wherever it was, there was a bed involved.

"Yes, ma'am." He tipped his cowboy hat.

"And where is that?" she asked, her voice as light as she could make it between gritted teeth as she struggled to restrain herself from out-and-out attacking him. What was wrong with her? Had seven years of abstinence taken their toll? Surely she was capable of controlling her baser instincts long enough to get through the rest of the evening. She feared her iron will and self-control were quickly ebbing away like sand beneath her feet at high tide.

"You'll see when we get there."

Excitement pooled low in her belly, making her

blood burn with the possibilities the evening might hold.

He drove away from Temptation on a highway headed north. After he'd gone what seemed like five miles, he turned off onto a dirt road.

As they bumped along, Gwen held on to the oh-shit handle above her head and laughed. "I'm beginning to wish I'd brought those jeans."

"I promise not to make you hike in those shoes."

"I'm going to hold you to that promise."

The dirt road wound through gnarled live oak trees and crossed a dry creek bed where Angus stopped the truck.

"This is the place?" Gwen asked, glancing out the window at an unremarkable scene barely illuminated by the stars shining overhead.

"Not quite." He twisted a knob on the dash. "Just shifting into four-wheel drive."

A nervous chuckle rose up her throat, escaping into the cab.

Angus shot her a look, his brows twisted. "Something funny?"

"Mona swore you wouldn't take me four-wheeling. I knew better."

He stepped on the accelerator and grinned. "You won't regret it."

Part of her already was, knowing the more time she spent with him, the worse it would be when she went back to Dallas, leaving him behind for good. After this one date, she wouldn't hold him to the others. Driving to and from Dallas every weekend would be too much trouble. He had his life, the ranch and his horses. She had Dalton, her business and soccer-mom duty.

But, for this one night, she could pretend it was just the two of them and a sky full of stars.

Angus drove up a steep hill.

Gwen held on, leaning forward to see what was on the other side of the hill. "We're not going to drive off a cliff, are we?"

"Not today," he assured her.

"Good, I didn't want to orphan Dalton because I went on a date."

"You worry about him, don't you?"

"I'm all he has." She stared at the dirt track ahead of them. "Mona's his godmother. If something happened to me, she'd take him."

"It's good to have backup."

The truck topped the hill and the view took Gwen's breath away. "Wow. You know how to pick the spots."

The hilltop was a mesa, overlooking the valley and a small lake reflecting the moonlight off its surface like a silvery path to heaven.

Angus switched on the radio and tuned to a country-western station. "Come on." He pushed open his door and climbed down.

"Really? You said I wouldn't have to hike."

"I said I wouldn't make you hike. I also promised I'd take you dancing. I live up to my promises." He rounded the truck and opened her door.

When she started to step down, he wrapped his big hands around her waist and lifted her out, settling her on her feet. Then he took her hands in his, settled one on his shoulder and clasped the other. The moonlight softened his rugged features with an indigo-blue tint. If possible, he was even more handsome than the first time they'd met.

She moved in his arms and smiled up at him. "They're playing a waltz."

"Perfect," he said, drawing her closer, his feet barely moving.

"The music?"

"No." He abandoned her hand and dragged her body against his. "You."

She stiffened, resisting, for a moment, the magnetic attraction of the cowboy who'd won her heart so many years ago. How could it be they'd ended up in the same saloon on the same night? What were the odds she'd come to Temptation and he'd be up for auction at the Annual Cowboy Auction?

"What made you want to be one of the cowboys auctioned off? It doesn't seem like something the old Angus I knew would ever consider."

"And I wouldn't have if my mother hadn't set me up."

"How did she get you to go to the Ugly Stick Saloon on ladies' night?"

He didn't say anything, but his arms tightened around her. "What's it matter? I was there, you were there. Now we're here. Let's dance."

She laid her cheek on his chest and listened to the beat of his heart, hammering fast and hard. If she wasn't mistaken, he was holding back, not telling her something she suspected was important.

The music played on, his body was warm against

hers and she relaxed, inhaling the scent of Angus. She'd give herself this night. One for the memories she'd have to be satisfied with until Dalton graduated high school and she could think of a life for herself.

Gwen slipped her arms around Angus's waist and leaned into him, absorbing his heat, her body generating more on its own. The moon and stars were doing their job and the music sealed the deal. It was a night to rekindle an old flame.

Beware your heart.

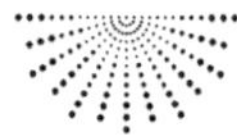

*A*ngus basked in the honeysuckle perfume of her hair. He threaded his hands through Gwen's thick riot of curls, stirring up more of the intoxicating scent. Then slid his hands down to her middle, across her naked back, the plunging neckline of the dress making it all too easy to touch her silken skin. How easy it would be to slide the straps over her shoulders. The dress would glide over her body and pool around her waist. A quick flick on the zipper would send it floating to the ground around those sexy stilettos.

He brushed his lips across her temple and prayed for patience, something his body seemed short on. Like a stallion sniffing a mare in heat, he wanted to bust through fences and take her as his.

Through years of taming skittish fillies, he'd honed his craft and now drew on that knowledge to woo this beauty back to his arms for good.

Cupping the back of her head, he tipped her face to the moonlight and drank in her features. "You're even more beautiful than the first time we made love."

"You're not half bad yourself." She traced the lines beside his eyes with the tip of her finger. "A few more wrinkles."

He wished he had all those years back that they'd lost between them. "I'm getting older."

"More distinguished," she corrected.

"That's what women say when they really mean old." He bent to nibble at her earlobe.

"And you've had many women say you look distinguished?" She tipped her head to the side, giving him free rein to trail his lips along her long, slender neck.

"Only you," he responded, his breath stirring tendrils of hair across her skin.

"Uh-huh." Gwen captured his cheeks in her palms and forced him to look at her. "Are you going to kiss me properly, or do I have to ask again?"

He stared at those full, lush lips, enjoying the way they pouted when she didn't get what she wanted. Especially when what she wanted was him. "Do you want me to kiss you?"

Her gaze fell to his lips, and he could see her answer before she spoke in a soft whisper that stirred his blood more than making love. "Yes. More than I want to take my next breath."

Her words lit a fire deep inside Angus and it exploded within, his senses flaming to life. He crushed her to him, curved his hand behind her head and kissed her like it would be the last kiss he'd get before the world ended.

When he broke away, he struggled to regain control, realizing he would lose that battle. "You can say no now, and I'll walk away. But, by God, if you say yes, there's no going back. I can't resist you anymore."

Gwen's nostrils flared and her eyes darkened. For a long moment she stood in the moonlight, her gaze locked with his. Then she dragged in a shuddering breath and pushed aside one strap of her dress, exposing a shoulder. The strap slid lower, revealing one full breast, the nipple already tight and distended.

Angus held her hips, pressing his rock-hard cock against her soft belly. He reached up to slide the other strap off her other shoulder, and watched as it slid over her skin and down to her waist where the skirt fit snugly on her hips. She hadn't been wearing a bra and nothing but the moonlight covered her skin, giving it a soft-blue tone, caressing her breasts with the cool color.

He slipped his hands over her bottom and down the back of her thighs, then lifted her.

Gwen wrapped her legs around his waist and took off his cowboy hat, throwing it through the open window of the truck. Then she threaded her fingers through his hair and leaned close to take his mouth with hers, darting her tongue past his teeth to connect with his. Her naked breasts pressed against his chest, heating his skin through the fabric of his shirt.

The rush of blood to his groin nearly crippled him as he strode with her to the rear of the truck. He popped the catch on the tailgate and lowered it with one hand

and then perched her bottom on the edge, stepping between her thighs.

She cradled his head in her hands and drew him to her breasts.

He took one of the turgid peaks between his teeth and flicked his tongue across the nipple.

Gwen gasped and arched her back, offering more.

He accepted, drawing her into his mouth, sucking hard on the nipple and twirling his tongue around the areola. Angus slipped his hands beneath her skirt and skimmed them up the outsides of her thighs.

Spreading her legs wider, she grasped one of his big hands and guided his fingers to her center, pressing one long digit into her dripping channel.

Ah, she was so wet for him. Angus's control shredded. He hooked a finger around her panties, dragged them down her legs and threw them over his shoulders.

Gwen grabbed for his belt buckle, ripping it loose, then struggled with the top button on his jeans.

Angus brushed her hands aside and ripped the line of buttons open. His cock spilled out into her hands, her warm fingers wrapping around his hard length.

"Hold that thought." Scooting to the edge of the tailgate, she dropped to the ground, landing smoothly on her stilettos.

"Are we done?" The thought of blue balls made him cringe.

"Not hardly." She flicked the buttons of his shirt open all the way down his front and pushed it over his shoulders. Once his chest was bared to the moonlight, she trailed her fingers across the muscles between his small brown nipples. Leaning forward, she captured his left nipple between her teeth and bit down softy.

He jerked back. "Hey. Those are attached."

"Umm. I know." She sank lower, settling onto her knees, trailing her tongue and lips across his torso and abdomen stopping when she reached his stone-hard shaft jutting straight out.

Angus moaned as she took him into her mouth, teasing the rounded head of his cock with the tip of her tongue, darting into the small hole at the center already dripping come.

She took the hooded bulb into her mouth and sucked gently.

Angus surged forward, unable to resist the animal inside.

Her jaw adjusted to his girth, accepting him, taking in his full length until he bumped against the back of her throat.

"Sweet Jesus, Gwen." Threading his fingers into her hair, he guided her head back and forth to match his thrusts into her wet, hot mouth.

The faster he thrust, the hotter he became. His body tensed. If he continued down this path, he'd come in her mouth. Angus jerked back, gripped her arms, pulled her up his body and lifted her to sit on the tailgate.

Without missing a beat, she wrapped her legs around him and drew him close by pressing her heels into his buttocks.

"Uh-uh." Angus shook his head. "My turn."

"Your turn?" she gasped.

"I want you ready."

"Any more ready and I'll explode."

"That's my line. Trust me, you aren't there yet." He pulled her to the edge of the tailgate and dropped to his knees between her legs.

The first time he tongued her clit, her body spasmed and she cried out, "Holy hell." She reached for his head and pulled it back to her. "Again."

This time he slipped a finger into her channel as he stroked the tightly strung bundle of nerves.

Her fingers curled into his scalp and her thighs squeezed against his ears. "Sweet Jesus, Angus. You're setting me on fire."

He blew a stream of warm air over her heated center.

"I need you inside me," she moaned.

"Not yet."

"Yes yet," she said, pulling his hair in an attempt to bring him up.

He flicked her clit and dove in to swirl, tease and relentlessly torment her.

Her body tensed, she dragged in a ragged breath and let out a long, sexy groan. "Oh. My. God. Angus. You're fuckin' killin' me." Her body convulsed and her hips jerked each time he touched her.

"I can't believe you still talk dirty during sex." Angus slipped another finger inside her channel, then another, stretching her, preparing her.

"Okay, okay. You have to come inside me now. I don't know if I can live through much more."

He chuckled and rose to his feet, pressing his cock to her entrance.

"Oh fucking hell!" Gwen cried out, and not in a good way.

Her expletive jerked Angus off course. "Did I hurt you?"

"No." Her brows dipped in a V. "I forgot the damned condoms. Mona gave me a month's supply, and I didn't have time to put them in my purse."

"I've got it covered." Angus reached into his back pocket for his wallet, his hands shaking with the intensity of his need. When he finally found the single condom he kept inside, he held it up. "Is this what you were looking for?"

"Yes." She snatched it from his fingers, tore it open and rolled it down over his cock. "Now, please, come into me now."

He obliged, her desperate cries more than he could handle. Angus drove into her, thrusting long, hard and all the way home, his balls slapping against her bottom.

"Again." She threaded her thumbs in his belt loops and dragged him out then back in again, pulling so hard he rammed into her.

Angus slid in and out, banging harder and harder until his nerves all lit on fire and exploded, sending him rocketing into orbit. He thrust one last time and held her against him, his fingers digging into her rounded ass.

For a long moment he stood in the moonlight reliving every wet dream he'd had of Gwen for the past seven years. When he came back to earth and reality, he captured her face in his hands and kissed her tenderly, brushing his lips across hers, sucking her lower lip between his. When he let go, he leaned his forehead against hers. "Want to lie out and watch for shooting stars?"

"No," she said, her voice shaky, her eyes downcast.

"What's wrong?"

"Nothing." A tear slipped down her cheek, the moonlight glinting off the moisture.

Angus brushed his thumb across Gwen's skin, capturing the tear. "Then why the tears?"

"It's nothing. We should go."

He drew out of her, disposed of the condom and tucked himself into his jeans. Then he pulled her straps back up over her shoulders, straightened her skirt over her thighs and rested his hands on her knees. "You want to talk about this nothing that's making you cry?"

"Not really." She slid off the tailgate and onto her feet. "I'm just really tired."

It was more than that, but damned if he knew what had gone wrong when everything had felt so incredibly good, and natural and right. This was where they were supposed to be. In each other's arms, not living separate lives.

He'd never stopped loving Gwen. That was why he hadn't been interested in dating, why he'd buried himself in the ranch and working with the horses. He'd been trying to get over his broken heart.

Now…

She was here. They'd made love. He refused to think they would go their separate ways. How could he let her go again?

He couldn't. It would kill him.

GWEN SAT in silence the entire ride down the hill, along the bumpy dirt road and all the way back to Temptation. When they arrived at the bed-and-breakfast, she got down from the truck before Angus could come around and assist her. She was afraid if she let him touch her again, she would completely fall apart.

And she didn't have the luxury of falling apart this time. Dalton was her world. Her focus had to be on providing him a loving home until he was grown and living on his own. Until then, she had to walk away from what her own heart yearned for, the overwhelmingly beautiful thing she and Angus had just shared.

Angus reached for her arm, but she stepped away. "I can see myself to my door. No need for you to stay."

"I'm not leaving until I know you're safely inside."

She stiffened, hardening her heart to what she couldn't have. "I live on my own in Dallas. I know what to look out for, how to take care of myself."

"So? You're not in Dallas. You're here with me," he said between gritted teeth. "I'm taking you up to your room."

Without responding, she turned and marched toward the house, entering the lobby. She hurried up the steps, almost running by the time she reached the top. Angus kept pace, no matter how fast she moved. His longer legs took the steps two at a time to her one.

Gwen didn't know why she was running. No matter how fast she moved she couldn't hide from her feelings for this tall, strong cowboy. Her first and only love.

At the top of the stairs, she dug in her purse for the key and dropped everything. When she bent to pick up her things, Angus bent too, their heads bumping.

He reached out and steadied her. "Are you all right?"

Hell no, she wasn't all right. Her heart was breaking into a million pieces and she didn't know how to make it stop. "I'm fine." She found the key, opened the door and fell inside.

Before she could close it behind her, Angus stuck his foot inside and grabbed her arm, dragging her up against him. "Tell me what's wrong. I'll fix it."

"Nothing's wrong. You're freakin' perfect," she said, her voice catching on a sob and locking down her throat. "It's me. I can't do this again. I can't fall in love with you knowing we won't be together."

"What the hell are you talking about?" He shook her gently. "We'll be together."

"We can't," she said. "I live in Dallas. I have Dalton. You and me…we just were never meant to be together."

"Bullshit." His fingers tightened on her arms. "We were meant to be together. If ever there was a reason to believe in fate, it was last night at the Ugly Stick Saloon."

She shook her head, tears streaming down her cheeks. "No. Fate teased us again. She brought us back together, knowing I couldn't stay and you couldn't leave what you have here. Dalton is my life. He's all I have, and I'm all he has. I won't force someone else on him or him on someone else because of my selfishness. Just leave."

"I'll leave for now, but this isn't over. It's far from

over." A ruddy flush rose up in Angus's cheeks. "Because, you see, I'm a McFarlan and McFarlans don't give up on the ones they love. Do you know what that means?"

By now Gwen was sobbing, shaking her head as she stood before him, her world coming apart, her heart breaking.

"It means," he said, "that I love you, and I'll be damned if I let you get away again. I will be back and I'll, by golly, woo you until you can't say no. You can't shut me out of your goddamned life." He yanked her into his arms and kissed her hard. Then he shoved her away from him and left, stomping down the steps and all the way out to his truck.

Gwen stood staring at the door, her heart squeezing hard, the pain so intense it almost brought her to her knees. Tears flowed down her face in an unending stream. She crumpled to the ground and curled into a fetal position, wrapping her arms around her knees, the dress swirled around her hips, her lack of panties a vivid reminder of the beauty of what she'd just experienced.

How could she push him away? It had to be the stupidest thing she'd ever done in her life. On the other hand, how could she expect Angus to take her and Dalton into his life? What man would understand that her son would always come first, and the man's needs would always be second?

A soft knock on the door barely penetrated the darkness of the hell she'd sentenced herself to.

"Gwen? It's me. Mona. Let me in. You promised me all the details."

"I don't feel like it," Gwen moaned from her position curled up on the floor.

"Gwen? What's wrong? Open the damn door." Mona banged louder.

If Gwen didn't answer the door, Mona would wake the other residents in the building.

Gwen pushed to her feet, wishing the floor would open up and swallow her so that she didn't have to take another breath that only made her hurt worse. Then she thought of Dalton. She had to keep moving for him.

Gwen twisted the doorknob and stood back.

Mona burst through, took one look at her and engulfed her in a huge hug. "What did he do? Was he hateful? I'll send Grant after him. Hell, I'll kill him myself."

"No." Gwen laughed, the sound coming out of her throat on a sob. "He was…perfect."

"Are those tears of joy?" Mona brightened, then her face fell. "Not with that look on your face. You resemble a kicked puppy." Her friend smoothed the damp hair out of her face. "Tell me what happened."

Blubbering like a fool, Gwen gave Mona the lowdown on what happened, skipping much of the sexy details. When she finished, her tears had dried, but her heart still hurt.

Mona crossed her arms and glared at her. "For a corporate-savvy woman with a great company and clients who swear by your business acumen and intelligence, you're pretty damned stupid sometimes."

Gwen reeled back as if she'd been slapped. "Mona, I thought you understood."

"I understand that you're being stupid." She cocked her head to the side. "Do you love the man?"

"We can't be together." Gwen swallowed in an attempt to clear the lump lodged in her throat. "How I feel has nothing to do with it."

"Like hell it doesn't." She stared hard at Gwen. "Do you love the man?"

"The sex was incredible, but I have to think about Dalton."

"Pull your head out of your panties. Do you fuckin' love the man?" Mona persisted.

"Yes." Gwen threw her hands in the air. "I never *stopped* loving him. All these years, I haven't thought of anyone else. There. Are you satisfied?"

Mona's face softened. "Then cut you and him a break, sweetie. Don't throw away something beautiful because you're afraid."

"I'm not afraid. I can't do this to Dalton."

"Bullshit." Mona shook her head, her look softening her words. "Dalton would love having Angus in his life."

"Maybe, but Angus could never love Dalton as much as I do."

"How do you know? You haven't even given the man a chance. You pushed him away as soon as it started getting hot."

"*After* it got hot," Gwen corrected.

"Right. Which is even worse. You led Angus on by making him believe you had feelings for him." Mona held Gwen's hands in hers. "Did you ever think that by pushing him away, you'd break *his* heart? Again?"

"Oh God." Gwen buried her face in her hands and tears sprang to her eyes. "No matter what I do, someone is going to get hurt."

"Not if you let Angus in. You win, he wins. Dalton gets a great man as a father." Mona spread her arms, palms up. "You'd have a complete family."

All her fears for the future, her mother-bear need to protect her son and her own raging desires piled in on her, swirling in her normally structured head. "I can't do this. I can't think about this right now."

"Meanwhile, you let Angus get away. The man who admitted he hasn't stopped loving you. The man you admitted you haven't stopped loving. Geez, Gwen, wake up. You don't get second chances like this every day."

A knock on the door jerked Gwen's attention away from Mona. Had Angus returned? Was he there to sweep her into his arms and smooth away all her doubts?

"Answer it." Mona pointed to the door, her jaw set firm. "It's probably Angus, come back to call bullshit at what you just did. You better answer that door, take him into your arms and tell him you love him before you lose him again."

Gwen took one step, then another. The next thing she knew, she was flying toward the door, her heart in her throat, hope surging out of control.

"Angus, I'm so sor—" she cried as she flung open the door. Gwen stopped dead in her tracks, her mouth falling open as she stared at the man leaning against the doorframe.

"Hey Gwendy baby, how's my favorite girl?" Wayne Kent, her ex-husband and the father of her little boy, strode through the door like he owned the place and turned. "Where's my kid? I've come to take custody of him."

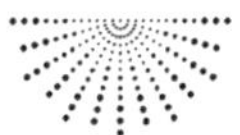

CHAPTER NINE

Gwen's belly cratered all the way to hell. Could he do that? Did Wayne have any rights where Dalton was concerned?

Fuck no!

"What do you mean, you've come to take custody? Dalton is *my* son. You've never shown one iota of interest in him."

"Well, I am now." He put his hands together and cracked his knuckles. "So? Where is he?"

"Who the hell are you?" Mona asked.

Gwen glared at the man. "Mona, this is my son's biological father, Wayne Kent." Then, planting her fists on her hips, she glared at the man. "No court in this state will grant you custody of any kind since you spent the last five-and-a-half years ignoring your son." She prayed he would take her words as gospel, otherwise the man would take her to court, and she couldn't risk him getting his hands on Dalton.

"Why now?" Mona asked. "You stayed away all this time. Why show up on Gwen's doorstep now, at ten o'clock at night five-and-a-half years later?"

"Yeah," Gwen said. "And how the hell did you find me here?"

"Finding you was easy. Your housekeeper told me where you'd gone." He gave Gwen a sly smile. "She's a pretty little *mamacita*."

Anger burned up her neck and into her cheeks. "Stay away from Delores. She's going to college to be a nurse, and she doesn't need to get mixed up with a bastard like you."

"It's completely her choice." Wayne gave Gwen the charming smile he'd flashed at her over her third shot of tequila that night she and her friends had landed in Vegas. The fateful night she'd slept with the charming gambler.

She'd been flattered, and missing Angus so much it hurt. "Why are you here now? You can't possibly care about a boy you've never met."

"Because I finally caught up with you after that quickie divorce. All these years, I didn't know you had a kid. Now that I do, I want joint custody of him. So where is he?"

Gwen thanked the stars that had aligned for Dalton to take to the McFarlans so quickly and stay the night with them. Under no circumstances did she want Dalton to meet his biological father until Gwen knew the real reason for Wayne showing up in their lives now.

"You're looking pretty good after all these years,

Gwendy. Makes me wish I hadn't signed those divorce papers." Wayne moved around her like a circling vulture. "You know I've thought about you often after that weekend we spent together in Vegas."

"That's funny, I haven't thought about you at all." She wanted him out, but not before she discovered his reason for coming. It couldn't be Dalton. He'd never even seen his son.

"Oh come on, Gwendy, don't you remember how much fun we had getting married at that little chapel on the strip?" His voice slipped into that rough cowboy drawl that at one brief moment in her life had reminded her of Angus.

Not now. Knowing he'd only been out for a weekend fling, she couldn't recall why he'd reminded her of Angus at all. "I was young and had a few too many drinks. And it was just one weekend. Not anything worth talking about, or remembering, but for the lesson learned. And stop calling me Gwendy. It's not my name."

Wayne's gaze narrowed. "That weekend must have meant something to you if you had my kid."

Gwen inhaled and counted five before saying, "It meant the condoms you used weren't worth a damn."

"Had I known you had a kid, I'd have come sooner."

"He has a name, it's Dalton. And I notified you of his birth with a letter, the day after I had him."

Wayne raised his hands, palms up. "Well, I don't remember getting a letter telling me I had a kid."

"Yeah? Well, you signed for it. I sent it certified."

God, this was Gwen's worst nightmare. The one where someone stole her son away from her.

He shook his head. "Nope, it wasn't me. And that's what I'll tell the judge."

"Gambler, right?" Mona said, her gaze raking Wayne.

"Right." Wayne turned his charm on Mona. "How'd you guess?"

She smirked. "I can smell a gambler from a mile away. They kind of stink like bullshit." She shook her head. "Don't see what Gwen saw in you."

"Me either," Gwen agreed. "But then I wasn't seeing straight at the time. I was on a weekend bender trying to get over someone else."

"What do you really want?" Mona demanded.

Wayne's smile slipped and the slimy charm went with it. "I want to see my boy." Then his gaze slid over Gwen. "And maybe rekindle an old flame."

"Nope." Gwen shook her head. "That's not going to happen when there wasn't a flame to begin with."

"How do you know?" Wayne rubbed a finger along her bare arm. "I usually have girls lining up to be with me."

"That's it." Mona stepped between Wayne and Gwen, and jabbed a finger toward the door. "Out of here. Now."

Wayne cocked his head to the side, his brows rising in challenge. "Or what? You'll call the police?"

Mona snorted and leaned into Wayne's face, her voice dropping to a threatening tone. "No, I'll call the biggest, meanest cowboy I know to take care of you and dump your sorry ass in a freshly dug hole so deep in the boondocks the authorities will never find you."

Wayne's eyes narrowed and he stared at Mona for a long time.

Gwen almost laughed when the badass gambler backed down and headed for the door. "I'm leaving, but I'll be back with a lawyer and a court order."

"You won't be back with shit," Mona said. "You're too much of a coward."

Wayne's lips pulled back in a snarl. "Shut your mouth, bitch. That kid's mine, and I'll see him when I like, and teach him how to gamble if that's what I want." He faced Gwen. "If you don't like it—tough. You, with all your money, makeup company and fancy cars, won't be able to do a damn thing about it."

Gwen stepped up to the bastard. "What is it you really want, Wayne? My money?"

"Is that it?" Mona stood beside Gwen. "Because, if it is, you're not getting squat out of Gwen. She *earned* her money, not by threatening single mothers."

Wayne fisted his hands and stepped toward Mona.

Gwen's pulse leaped and she moved between the two. "Leave, Wayne."

He breathed through his nose like an angry bull. "I'm going, but I'll be back with a court order." He left, slamming the door behind him.

Gwen sank into one of the lounge chairs and buried her face in her hands. "Damn, damn, damn."

"What are you worried about?" Mona stroked her hair. "That man doesn't have a leg to stand on."

"I've seen it happen all too often. A woman goes

into court thinking she has all her cards lined up and then bam. The court gives the deadbeat joint custody. A boy needs a father figure, they'll say. No matter how bad a role model the dad is." Gwen looked up at Mona, her vision blurred by the tears threatening to overflow. "Dalton doesn't even know the man. Can you imagine Wayne marching in and taking Dalton away for court-ordered visitation? What if he never brought him back?" Gwen shook her head. "I can't let that happen."

"We'll get a good lawyer," Mona said. "One of the best."

"What if it's not good enough? What if I get a judge sympathetic to the father? What if he believes Wayne wasn't informed of Dalton's birth?" Gwen stood and paced across the room and back. "Dalton would be terrified. And Wayne is not fit to be a parent."

Mona snorted. "He's not fit to be a human."

Gwen turned around. "Unzip me."

"Why?" Mona frowned and didn't move to comply.

"I need to go get Dalton."

"Now? He's probably asleep out at the ranch."

"I have to get him." Gwen twisted around, reaching for the zipper. "I couldn't sleep with Wayne out there. What if he tries to kidnap Dalton?"

"Like I said, I'll find the biggest, baddest cowboy out there to lynch the bastard. Grant would stand first in line. He loves Dalton. Then I'd take my turn and chop off Wayne's balls, if he has any." Mona stood in her black jeans, black boots and a soft-pink tank top, her curly blond hair pulled up in a loose ponytail. She looked like an avenging dark angel who could kick ass and hand out cotton candy to the spectators.

Gwen couldn't ask for a truer friend. "I can't let you do that. If it's money Wayne wants, I'll give it to him. Anything to keep from losing Dalton."

"Oh, honey, you can't do that. You give a man money once, and he'll be back again and again. It's like feeding a bear. He'll quit trying to feed himself."

"This bear is Dalton's biological father. He has rights."

Mona's lips pressed into a line. "He lost those rights the day he ignored your certified letter."

"Still, I can't relax until I know Dalton is safe." She twisted again, reaching for the zipper.

A loud knock sounded on the door and Gwen froze, her fingers on the zipper tab, her desperation spiking into raw, raging anger. "Go away, you self-centered bastard!" she yelled, too distraught to think straight.

She listened for the sound of footsteps, but only got silence. "I mean it. Get lost!" Her voice caught on a sob.

"I'll handle this." Mona started for the door.

"No. Let me." Gwen reached for the doorknob and flung it open. "What part of get lost did you not—" She stopped and stared at the big cowboy standing in the doorframe, his hat in his hands, a frown denting his beautiful brow.

"I admit I'm clueless when it comes to women. Did I do something heinous to piss you off?" he asked, his fist wrapped around his hat's brim. "I'll leave, just as soon as you hear me out." He stared into her face, his jaw tight, the light shining from his eyes fierce. "I love you, Gwendolyn Graves, and I'm not going to leave you alone until you admit you love me too. Do you hear me? I love you."

Gwen sniffed once, twice, and flung herself into his arms, holding on to him as if he were the life raft in a stormy sea. "Oh, Angus. I love you."

Angus chuckled. "You're booting me out one minute and hugging me tight the next." He held her with one hand and smoothed her hair with the other. "Either you're bipolar or I won't ever understand the workings of a woman's mind."

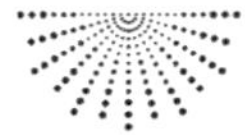

$\mathcal{A}$ngus wasn't sure if he was coming or going where Gwen was concerned. He'd come back determined to shake some sense into her and force her to admit she still had feelings for him.

When she'd yelled at him through the door, telling him to go away, his heart had dropped like a lead weight into his belly. He'd stood there in shock, his feet refusing to move. Then she'd thrown open the door, cussing him one second and hugging him the next.

"So what's it to be? Are you going to throw me out again, or can I come in?"

She raised her head, tears swimming in her eyes, with traces on her face, leaving tiny, shiny tracks across her skin. "Oh, Angus."

Not the answer he was looking for, but he couldn't argue with the fact he was holding her in his arms again. And damn, it felt good to hold Gwen, even as she soaked his best shirt with a flood of tears. And damn that dress. As pretty as she looked in it, the garment only made him want to rip it off her and make love to her into the small hours of the morning.

"Ahem. Just so you know, I can't get out with you two standing in the way." Mona grinned. "I could stand here and watch this touching reunion, or you could let me squeeze by and leave you two alone."

Gwen pushed away from Angus and smoothed the front of her dress, tears falling onto her hands. "I'm sorry. I was just going to call and tell you I would be picking up Dalton tonight." Her voice broke and she refused to look him in the eye.

"Why?" Angus tipped her chin up and his chest tightened at the hazel eyes full of tears. "Babe, what's wrong?"

She only shook her head, the tears sliding down her cheeks.

Angus pulled her back against him and held her, his heart breaking along with whatever was breaking hers.

"I'll just be going now." Mona attempted to squeeze by them.

"What happened here?" Angus asked.

"Gwen can tell you all about it." Mona made it past them and through the door. "But if a slick, blond cowboy with a belt buckle bigger than his dick shows up, shoot him."

Gwen laughed, her fingers digging into Angus's shirt. "Mona, you don't have to go."

Mona called out, "Oh yes I do, sweetie. You can thank me later."

Angus edged Gwen into the room and closed the door behind them. "Okay, now tell me what's going on."

"I don't want to go into it." She stepped away and scrubbed tears from her eyes with the back of her hand. "You couldn't do anything about it anyway."

"I might be just a cowboy, but I'm smarter than I look." He winked. "Try me."

"No, really. I have to go." She glanced around the room, her gaze seeming to roam without purpose. "I need to go pick up Dalton."

"He and Colin would be heartbroken if you picked him up now. They have the entire living room converted into Fort McFarlan and when I left earlier, they were laying siege on Mom's stash of cookies."

Gwen laughed, hiccupped and dropped her hand to her side. "This is all so messed up."

"Seriously, trust me. I'm pretty good at turning things around." And he hated seeing her cry. It was tearing him up inside.

"It's my business. Not something you need to worry about." She pushed out of his arms, turned to gather her purse in her hand and slipped her feet into the strappy black stilettos. "Look, Angus, you don't have to go through with any more dates, and I doubt I'll come back to Temptation anytime soon. We should say goodbye now and forget this weekend ever happened."

He grabbed her hand and made her stop what she was doing and focus on him. "We made a deal. Eight dates. We shook on it. I'm not reneging and neither are you. Something's got you scared. Whatever it is can be fixed."

"I'm not so sure."

"Sweetheart, you're not alone anymore. I'm here. I can help." He tipped her chin up. "If you let me."

Gwen pushed her hair back from her forehead and sighed. "Fine. Remember Dalton's father who wasn't in the picture?"

Angus frowned. "Yeah."

Those tears welled again. "Well, he's just decided to be in the picture."

"When?"

"He left a few minutes before you came back."

Angus's fist clenched. "What did he want?"

"Custody of Dalton." Her voice wobbled. "Dalton's never met the man. He'd be so afraid to go with him." Gwen bit down on her trembling bottom lip.

"Are you telling me his father didn't know about him until now?"

"No. I notified him with a certified letter when Dalton was born, and told him in that letter that I didn't expect anything from him. He never responded. All I got was the signature card in the mail that he'd received the letter."

"You didn't have any legal documentation drawn up granting you sole custody or anything?"

"I didn't think I had to. Wayne never made a claim." She gulped. "Until tonight. He's threatening to sue for custody. I think he really wants money, not custody."

"Bastard." Angus wished the man were there so that he could wrap his hands around the man's throat and squeeze until he turned blue. Any man who used a child to blackmail a woman should be strung up the nearest tree.

"I need to get to my son." She tried to shake Angus's hand off her arm. "What if Wayne tries to take Dalton from me?"

"He won't. Colin and my mother are with Dalton right now. He's safe and I doubt Wayne will find him at the ranch." Angus stroked his hands down Gwen's arms. "Babe, he's in the safest place possible."

"Are you sure?" She looked up at him, her eyes swimming again. "I don't know what I'd do without Dalton. He's the only family I have."

"What about your parents? Where are they now?"

"They died in an auto accident a couple months before Dalton was born."

"I'm sorry to hear that."

"What am I going to do?"

"You're going to come home with me."

"Yes." She nodded. "To get Dalton. I'll drive back to Dallas tonight."

"No," Angus said, shaking his head. "You're going to come stay at the ranch tonight. I have a friend who could recommend a really good child-custody lawyer."

"Thanks, Angus, but I can contact my corporate lawyer and get a recommendation for an attorney in Dallas. I can take care of this myself. I'm sorry I fell apart all over you." She gave him a crooked smile that melted his knees and made him want to hold her and never let her go again.

"If I didn't want you to fall apart on me, I'd have told you." He held on to her hand, refusing to release her, afraid that if he did he'd lose her forever. "Let me bear some of your burden. I'm strong. I can handle it. Besides, Dalton's a neat kid. I'd help you out just for his sake, even if I didn't love you as much as I do."

"I should go back to Dallas," she said, her voice quavering.

"You're not going back now. It's too late." He led her toward her suitcase and threw her belongings in one-handed, still holding on to hers. "You're coming home with me, and we'll work this out together."

For a moment she watched. Then she shook her head. "Okay. I'll come with you. If you'll let me have my hand, I'll get my things from the bathroom."

Angus gently squeezed her fingers. "As long as you don't try to make a run for it. You're done running."

"Yes, sir." She gave him a watery smile and hurried to pack her toiletries, adding them to the jumble of clothes in her suitcase. Less than five minutes later, they climbed into his truck, leaving her Cadillac behind.

Angus's heart swelled. It felt like he was bringing Gwen home for good. He had no doubt there would be trouble in the near future, but he hoped this would be the first step toward the rest of their lives together.

WHEN ANGUS PULLED up to the ranch house, Gwen didn't wait for him to open her door or help her down. She slipped from the truck and hurried toward the house, anxious to see for herself that her son was okay.

With Wayne in the area, she didn't trust him to leave her son alone.

Angus removed her suitcase from the backseat, followed her up the porch steps and then reached around her to slip his key into the lock.

Inside, the house was dark except for a soft lamp lit in the living room. Blankets were strung from one piece of furniture to the next in an impressive array covering the majority of the room.

"Hey, I didn't expect you two to come back tonight." Colin rolled out from under the tent and pushed to his bare feet.

"Where's Dalton?" Gwen asked.

"He's fast asleep inside." Colin smiled and held up the edge of a blanket. "See for yourself."

Gwen squatted beside the fort and peered inside.

Dalton lay curled up on a sleeping bag, a pillow beneath his head, a smile playing at his lips.

Relief filled Gwen and she straightened, unwilling to wake her son from such a sound sleep, nor did she have a good reason to.

"He and I had a lot of fun, and we even snagged some of Mom's best cookies. All in all, it was a good time." Colin nodded. "That's a great kid you got there."

"Thanks." Gwen smiled.

"No. Thank you for sharing him with ol' Uncle Colin." He puffed out his chest and grinned. "I kind of like the sound of that—Uncle Colin." Angus's brother winked. "Now, if you'll excuse me, I promised Dalton I'd spend the night in the fort." The man stretched. "I have to admit, it was a lot easier sleeping on the floor when I was Dalton's age."

"Then let me," Gwen suggested. Colin had already done so much to make Dalton's stay fun and exciting.

Colin frowned. "No way. This hero-worship thing is addictive. I wouldn't want Dalton to think I bailed on him in the middle of the night." Colin ducked beneath the blankets. "Good night, you two."

Gwen's belly tightened as Angus led her down the dark hallway to a room on the right and switched on the light. "This is Brody's old room. He lives in Seattle right now, though Colin is working on getting him to come home."

The room was painted in a soft gray-blue. The large, queen-sized bed draped with a brown-, navy- and cream-colored quilt took up much of the space. Photographs lined the wall, all lovingly framed and tastefully placed, Gwen assumed by their mother. They were photos of a boy growing into a man. Some were taken in sports uniforms, others were of him and his brothers laughing and smiling for the camera, wearing jeans and freshly pressed shirts as if they were going to church.

"My room is directly across the hall. Colin's is the next one over and Mom has the room at the end. She used to be a light sleeper when we were teens, but she can sleep through almost anything now that we're grown and not trying to sneak out."

Gwen paused in the doorway, her hand on the knob, her teeth chewing on her lower lip.

Angus pulled her into the safety of his embrace. "Everything is going to be all right."

"I hope so." Gwen laid her cheek against his chest,

inhaling the fresh outdoorsy, masculine scent that was all Angus. Her fingers curled into his shirt and she held on. "Would your mother be shocked if you stayed in here with me?"

A soft snort stirred the hair at her temple. "I guarantee she'd be fine with it. She'd wish for me to be happy. And being with you makes me happy."

He smoothed his hand over her hair and backed her into the room, closing the door behind him.

"What about Dalton?" Gwen asked, undoing the buttons on his shirt.

"As far as he knows, you're at the B and B in Temptation." Angus pressed a finger to her lips to quell her next question. "I'll slip out before morning to make it easier for you."

She smiled up at him and tugged his shirt loose from his jeans. "Thank you."

"I'm glad you're still wearing this dress." He slipped one strap from her shoulder and let it fall to her waist. "I'll be even happier when you're wearing nothing at all."

"Then here, let me." She shrugged out of the other strap and let it drop to her waist. Her breasts shone in the light from the moon coming through the open blinds. "Maybe we should close those?" She nodded toward the window.

"No. I like seeing your skin bathed in nothing but moonlight." He reached behind her and unzipped the lower half of the dress and it floated to the floor, leaving her naked and tingling all over.

Gwen took a step back, giving him a full-length look

at her body, proud she'd kept her figure by working out five days a week. "You locked the door?"

Angus nodded, his nostrils flaring. He ripped his shirt off his shoulders and toed off his boots. "I'd say you haven't changed a bit, but you have."

Gwen frowned, her ego taking a hit. "Having a baby does that to a woman."

He ripped the buttons loose on his jeans and shoved them off, stepping free and naked to stand in front of her. Reaching out, he traced a finger along the side of her cheek, down the long line of her neck and across a breast. "You're even more beautiful than you were at twenty-one."

"My hips are bigger." Gwen held her arms up and swayed.

Angus caught her hips in his big hands. "They have a sexier curve."

"My breasts are fuller." She plumped her breasts, her back straight, her chin held high, happy she'd increased a cup size in the seven years and hadn't lost the perky bounce.

"More to love." Angus raised one hand to tweak a nipple.

Her heart light, she smiled and wound her fingers through his hair. "I like the way you think, cowboy."

"I love everything about you, babe." He bent to capture her mouth and kissed her, holding her body against his, his stiff cock pressing into her belly.

When they broke apart, Gwen took his hand and led him to the bed. She flung back the quilt and lay across the clean white sheets. "It's been seven years; we can't make up for lost time."

"No." Angus lay down beside her and brushed his fingers across her breast and down her belly to the apex of her thighs. "But we can try."

Gwen lay back, letting her knees fall open, her hand resting over her pussy, touching herself, liking how hot she was, amazed how much she wanted him. "Don't take it slow. I want you, Angus, and I don't want to wait to have you inside me."

In less than the time it took to say *take me*, he was leaning over her, kissing a path from her lips, across her breasts and down to the apex of her thighs, searing his mark into her skin and into her soul. This was where she'd always longed to be and now that she was here, she was exhilarated and afraid. Life had thrown her some curve balls and she didn't want this to be one of them.

Soon, she forgot everything in the pleasure he gave her. His fingers parted her folds and stroked her to a frenzy; then his tongue replaced his fingers and he lapped at her, swirling, flicking and nibbling at her clit until she pulled him up by the hair. "I can't wait any longer. I want you inside me. *Now.*" She pulled him into position.

He paused, his cock nudging her entrance. "Are you sure?"

"Never more so in my life." Almost past caring, she surfaced from her lust long enough to ask. "Do you have any protection?"

"Damn." Angus leaned across her, his chest rubbing

against her breasts, the hairs tickling and stimulating her nipples. He dug in the nightstand and held up a single foil packet. "I don't know how old this is."

"It'll do." She took it from him, rolled it over his full, thick shaft and then she guided him to her. "Give it to me, hard and fast."

He obliged, thrusting deep.

Her channel stretched deliciously, accommodating his length and thickness.

Then he moved in and out of her, pounding so hard the bed shook and banged against the wall.

Gwen giggled. On his next thrust, she forgot everything but the way he made her feel inside. She gripped his ass and held on for the ride, really happy for the first time in years. The tingling started at her center, building quickly until it exploded outward, firing off electrical bursts to the tips of her fingers and toes.

Angus bent to kiss her lips as he entered her one last time, driving all the way home. He held steady, his body rigid, his cock hard and throbbing, his breath catching and holding.

Gwen held on to the sensations as long as she could. When she came back to earth, she lay spent against the mattress, replete in the best sex ever, her eyes drifting closed. "Wow."

"Agreed." Rolling to his side, Angus trailed a finger over the swell of her breast. "Sleep, sweetheart. Tomorrow will be a better day."

"I don't know. It would have to top today. Kinda hard to beat." She slipped into a dark oblivion, barely aware when Angus left the bed.

CHAPTER ELEVEN

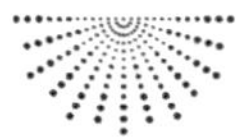

Angus checked the clock. For all that had happened so far that night, it was barely past eleven o'clock. Gathering his clothes, he crossed the hallway to his room, dressed and hurried to his study.

A few phone calls and he had a meeting set up at the Ugly Stick for midnight and another for early in the morning. Rather than hang around the house where temptation lay sleeping in Brody's old room, Angus left the ranch and headed for the saloon, ready to lay out a plan.

At a quarter 'til midnight, Angus pulled into the parking lot of the Ugly Stick Saloon. As he got out of his pickup, he heard a shout near the entrance. Two men were leading a third out the door between them. The man in the middle shook loose and fell to the ground. "I told you I'd get the goddamn money. I just need time."

"You're out of time, Kent. The boss wants his money now." The larger man kicked the man on the ground.

"Hey!" Angus shouted. "What's going on?"

"None of your damn business."

"Maybe not, but I know the owner of the Ugly Stick, and she wouldn't be too happy about whatever you're doing."

The big guy glared as Angus strode up to the group. "You'd do best to go inside and leave us alone."

"Yeah, well, that's not going to happen." Angus glanced from one man to the other.

Each man weighed a good fifty pounds more than he did and they were bulky, like bouncers at a Vegas club. With scarred faces and tattoos crisscrossing their arms, they'd scare a lesser cowboy.

"I'll tell you what I'll do," Angus said in his most congenial tone, adding a big stupid grin. "I'll go inside. But I'm taking this man with me."

The man on the ground rose to stand behind Angus. "Thanks, Mister."

"Don't thank me," Angus muttered. "We're not inside yet."

"Here's the deal," the guy with the skull tattoo said. "You can go in and leave the deadbeat with us."

"Sorry. I can't do that." Angus spread his arms wide. "So what next?"

"This." The big man took a swing with his ham hock of an arm.

Angus had expected it would come to violence, and he was ready. He easily ducked the swing, grabbed the arm and twisted it up behind the man's back between his shoulder blades. "Now, let me give you the deal again. You and your little friend will leave, while me and my new friend go inside. Got it, little big man?"

The other man lunged at Angus, but Angus spun, taking the one with the skull tattoo with him, ratcheting the man's arm higher up the middle of his back. "Tell him to back off, or I break your arm," Angus warned.

"Back off, Roland," Skull Tattoo grunted.

Roland, his fist raised, his attitude one of repressed anger, hesitated.

Angus nudged the arm again.

Skull Tattoo groaned. "Back the fuck off!"

His fists falling to his side, Roland took a couple of steps backward.

"Go inside," Angus ordered the man they'd been kicking around.

The man scurried to the door and disappeared inside without offering to assist Angus in disentangling himself from the two men.

Angus was all right with that. He didn't need the help. He backed away from Roland, still holding on to Skull Tattoo's arm. When he reached the door, he put his foot against the man's back and shoved hard, sending him flying forward, where he sprawled on the ground. Then he turned and entered as Greta Sue was exiting.

He caught Greta Sue's arm. "Just call the sheriff. Those two are big."

"They shouldn't be fighting on the premises." Greta Sue's face was set in grim, tight lines, like she wanted to chew them up and spit them out.

"Yeah, but unless we get backup, we'll be in a world

of hurt. They're a little more than either you or I can handle." He didn't tell her that he'd just handled them and they would be twice as mad and ready to hurt the next person out the door.

Audrey Anderson joined them at the door, her brow furrowed. "I called the sheriff. Are you okay, Angus?" She touched his arm and looked him over.

He grinned. "I'm fine. But I could do with a whiskey."

She smiled. "It's on the house."

He sat at the bar and Libby filled a glass with a double. The interior of the bar was a lot different than it had been twenty-four hours before. Gone were the masses of women and the few cowboys they were bidding on. The regulars were there, dancing with their girls, playing a hand of cards or just drinking beer and whiskey.

"Thanks, man. I would have been raw meat if you hadn't come along when you did." The man the two goons outside had kicked to the ground pulled up a stool beside Angus. He pressed a hand to his ribs, winced and stared at the glass in Angus's hand, his tongue running across his lips.

Angus held up his glass of whiskey. "Can I buy you a whiskey?"

He nodded. "Thanks. I'm short on cash."

Libby appeared in front of them and splashed whiskey into a glass and set it in front of the stranger.

"Why were they roughing you up?" Angus asked.

The man's lips pressed together. "Their boss thinks I owe him money."

Angus lifted his glass and took a pull before continuing with "And do you?"

Pushing a hand through dirty-blond hair, the man shrugged. "Yeah."

"A lot?"

Again, he shrugged. "Twenty grand."

Angus whistled. "I can see where their boss might be anxious to get it back."

"He can afford it." The man tossed back his whiskey and held it out for a refill. "I have a plan to pay him off by the end of the week."

"Must be a good one if you can come up with twenty grand in a hurry."

"My ex is loaded. I'm going to get her to loan me the money."

Angus's hand wrapped around his glass so tightly he thought it would break. He knew without asking who this deadbeat bastard was, and he wished he'd left him to the two men in the parking lot.

"Women can be hard to read," Angus managed to force out between his gritted teeth. "What makes you so sure she'll hand over that kind of money?"

"I hold the trump card." He grinned, displaying yellowing teeth and an evil glint in his eyes.

Dalton.

A sweet kid who only wanted to love and be loved. It took every ounce of restraint to keep from balling his fist and shoving it into the man's face.

"Libby, could we get another whiskey?" Angus called out.

While the bartender poured, Angus asked, "So what's this trump card?"

"The kid. All I have to do is pretend I want custody of the kid and she'll give me any goddamn thing I want."

Angus smiled up at Libby. "Hear that, Libby?" He turned to the man beside him. "Kent." He faced the man on the adjacent stool. "That's your name, right?"

He nodded. "Wayne Kent." He leered at Libby. "Prettiest bartender I've seen in a long time."

"Wayne says he can get a woman to do anything for him if he threatens to take custody of her kid. What woman would fall for that?"

Libby snorted. "Every woman I know, if the man has any legal claim."

Angus turned back to Wayne. "Seems your plan has merit. When are you putting the screws to her?"

Wayne swirled the whiskey in his glass. "I was thinking about tomorrow morning, before she leaves town to go back to Dallas."

Angus clapped a hand to Wayne's back. "Hey, buddy, let me help you out."

"No, no. I can't let you do that." Wayne waved a hand. "You've already done enough."

"Not nearly," Angus said, strengthening his resolve to make things right for Gwen. "Come on. I feel responsible, having saved your life once." Angus winked, hiding the anger simmering below the surface. "I know most of the people in town. I can set up a meeting place and let you take over."

"You'd do that?" He brightened. "Why?"

"I hate to see someone suffer."

"Thanks, but I'm not sure she'll answer my phone call. She was pretty mad at me last time I talked to her."

"Right. That would be a problem." Angus raised his brows. "Who is she?"

"Gwendolyn Graves. She's staying in the bed-and-breakfast on Main in Temptation."

"Gwen Graves?" Angus grinned. "This will be easier than I thought. I have it on good authority she's not staying at the B and B tonight, and that she might be a little more open to negotiation."

"You think? I don't know…" Wayne sighed, "…she was hot last time I talked to her."

Angus jotted his home phone number on a napkin and handed it to Wayne. "Dial this number. They'll be sure to get her to answer."

Libby stood behind the bar, her eyes narrowed, her mouth set in a grim line.

Angus shot her a glance and shook his head, the movement almost imperceptible if the person wasn't looking for it.

Libby nodded once and turned away.

Wayne tucked the napkin in his breast pocket. "You really know how to help a fellow out."

"Then it's a plan? I can get the keys to this bar. You can meet her here."

"That would be great. Hopefully, she can wire the money straight to my account."

"I'm sure it'll be that easy." Angus nodded. "Nine o'clock tomorrow morning, I'll make sure the door's unlocked. Now, if you'll excuse me. I'm calling it a night. Nice meeting you, Wayne."

"Same."

Angus stood.

"Hey." Wayne put his hand on Angus's arm. "Thanks, Mister…"

"Angus McFarlan."

"Thanks, Angus." He stuck out his hand and Angus shook it, forcing back the temptation to slug the guy in the face.

Angus left the bar, hooked Jackson Gray Wolf's arm and walked him out through the back door. "Thanks for meeting with me on short notice. Can you deliver Gwen's Cadillac to my house?"

Jackson nodded. "Sure. When do you need it?"

"Tonight, if that's possible. And, Jackson, you still interested in buying my stud?"

GWEN WOKE to the scent of bacon and biscuits wafting through the room. Her stomach grumbled and she stretched on the crisp white sheets, her hand reaching out for the man beside her.

A tap on the door made her jerk upright, draw the sheet up over her naked breasts and run a hand through her unruly hair. "Come in," she called out. Her heart raced and she held her breath, waiting for the man of her dreams to walk in and pick up where they'd left off the night before.

"I'm glad you decided to stay the night here instead of at the B and B." Mrs. McFarlan backed into the room, carrying a large tray loaded with heavenly smells.

Gwen yelped and flattened herself against the

mattress, pulling the sheet and quilt up over her naked body. "Mrs. McFarlan, I…didn't expect…" she bit the inside of her mouth and finished with, "…you to make a fuss."

The older woman turned with a wide grin. "We don't have guests often, so it's nice to make a fuss." Her gaze darted around the room. "Oh, I thought I heard… um…" She paused, her face falling. "Well, there's enough food here for two."

"Thank you, Mrs. McFarlan."

"Call me Maggie, or Mama Mac." She smiled. "I like the sound of that. I'm glad you and Angus worked things out. He's done nothing but mope around here for the past seven years."

Gwen's heart leaped and pounded against her ribs. Despite the fact she was hiding her naked body beneath the covers, she couldn't help questioning. "He moped?"

Maggie winked. "You know. Man-moping, when they get all dark and brooding all the time." Still carrying the loaded tray, she focused on Gwen. "Do you want me to plump your pillows so that you can sit up and I can put this tray in your lap?"

"No!" Gwen shook her head. "Thank you. If you could set it on the table over there, I'd appreciate it. I like to stretch and wake up slowly."

"Certainly. I suppose Angus got up early to feed the animals. I'll go check on our little man. He was polishing off a rather large stack of pancakes in the kitchen. I need to make sure Colin doesn't try to steal any." She winked. "I'm on strike as far as my boys are concerned. I'm glad to see Angus taking me seriously."

"On strike?" Gwen frowned.

"I'm not cooking, cleaning or running errands for them anymore, and I told them I'd sell the ranch if they didn't make an effort to find wives, settle down and have kids." She chuckled. "I didn't know how effective that threat would be, or I'd have made it a lot sooner." Maggie set the tray on the table and straightened. "Let me know if you need anything. I can loan you some clothes if you like. Though you're much taller than I am, I could probably come up with a dress or two."

Gwen sank deeper into the blankets. "No, thank you. I have my suitcase."

"Okay then. I'll leave you to get dressed." Mrs. McFarlan left the room, silence making the older woman's words echo in Gwen's head.

She'd told her sons she'd sell the ranch if they didn't find wives.

A sick, hollow sensation washed over her, making her stomach clench and her eyes sting.

All this time that she'd thought Angus had really missed her and wanted to be with her he'd been fulfilling his mother's demand to marry and have children.

What kind of fool was she to think her world could fall into place in less than two days?

Gwen lay still while her heart shattered into a million pieces. Her first jinclination was to pull the blanket up over her head, shrivel up and die. But she couldn't. She had to take Dalton back to Dallas and the life she'd built since she'd left Temptation the first time.

Pushing back the sheet and quilt, she struggled to sit

up and stand, the heavy weight of betrayal dragging her down. She trudged past the tray of food, so hopefully prepared, and sank to the floor in front of her suitcase, her eyes filling with tears.

How could she be so incredibly stupid? He didn't love her at all. He loved his horses and his ranch so much he'd marry her to keep it.

She fought to keep from shedding one more tear for Angus McFarlan. The man didn't deserve her or her tears. A single fat tear slipped from the corner of her eyes and started down her cheek. Gwen swiped at it, refusing to wallow, resisting the urge to sink into despair. She was a very successful business owner with people who looked to her for direction and a son she loved to the moon and back. So she was lonely. That would pass. Life went on.

Gwen swiped at the second tear and grabbed a pair of trousers, a blouse and her bra, dragging them on as quickly as she could. When she had fully dressed and brushed her hair back into a low ponytail, she zipped her suitcase and exited the room where she'd dared to dream of a future with a man who was only using her.

Dalton skipped down the hall, spotted her and ran all out, crashing into her empty gut. "Mama, can we stay here forever? I want to live on a ranch. This ranch. Memaw said I could have a puppy and a pony of my own. Uncle Colin said he'd show me how to throw a football and Angus said he'd teach me to ride my pony." He hugged her tight, his smile so wide it nearly blinded her. "Can we stay? Please?"

"Oh, Dalton." Her voice caught on the lump stuck in her throat. "We have to go home to Dallas."

"But I don't want to go to Dallas. Memaw said there's a school in town."

"But we don't live here, sweetheart." Gwen ruffled her son's head. "Go put your boots on. We need to leave."

A telephone rang somewhere in the house and Mrs. McFarlan's voice carried to where Gwen stood in the hall. "Gwendolyn Graves? Why yes. Just a moment, please." Angus's mother appeared at the end of the hallway. "There's a man on the phone for you, Gwen."

"Did he say who it was?"

"No, I don't recognize the voice." She glanced behind her. "Do you want me to ask?"

Gwen sighed. "No. I'll take it." The only people who might have guessed she'd ended up here would be Mona and Grant. Trudging down the hall, she turned toward the living area, dreading running into Angus. The telephone stood on a table in the hallway.

Gwen answered, "This is Gwen."

"Gwendy baby."

Just when Gwen thought her day couldn't get worse, it did. "What do you want, Wayne?"

"Ah, so glad I found you." He paused then said, "All I want is joint custody."

Gwen's stomach sank. "I'm not giving you joint custody," she said, her tone flat, unbending.

"I'll make this easy on you. All you have to do is show up at the Ugly Stick Saloon at nine o'clock and we can discuss the details."

"Wayne, who told you I was here?"

"A man who saved my ass last night at the bar gave me this number." Wayne chuckled. "He's a good guy. Knows a lot of people in this pissant town. He's the one who suggested we meet this morning. I'm sure you'll come to see reason."

Past her endurance, Gwen demanded, "Who told you I was here, Wayne?"

"His name is Angus McFarlan."

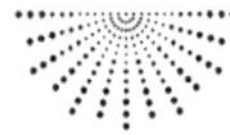

CHAPTER TWELVE

*A*ngus pulled a lot of people out of bed early on a Sunday morning, determined to get this party underway and everything in place before Wayne Kent and Gwen showed up at the Ugly Stick Saloon.

He'd stayed up into the small hours of the morning working with Mona, Grant and Sandy Jameson to get everything right. Libby would be there and Jackson and Audrey had insisted on showing up to let him in and provide moral support should things turn ugly.

Sandy was due to arrive ten minutes before nine, but she still hadn't arrived.

"Don't worry." Audrey laid a hand on his arm. "Everything is going to work out fine."

"I keep thinking I'm missing something."

"You've done the best you could in a very short amount of time."

Angus shook his head. "What if my best isn't good enough? What if Wayne doesn't go for it?"

"He will." Jackson slipped an arm around his pregnant wife. "The man has no other choice. I just got off the phone with Grant. Gwen dropped Dalton off five minutes ago. She should be here any minute."

Libby stood at the front entrance of the Ugly Stick Saloon. "A Cadillac just pulled into the parking lot."

Angus's heart slammed against his ribs. "I should have worked this out with Gwen before we decided to go through with this."

"You couldn't," Audrey said. "Her reactions to Wayne need to be sincere to make him feel like he's got her where he wants her."

Shaking his head, Angus wasn't so certain. "She doesn't like surprises where Dalton is concerned."

"It's too late now," Libby called out from across the room. "Here she comes."

"You'd better take your position." Audrey waved toward the hallway behind the bar. "Jackson and I are right behind you."

"Where the hell is Sandy?"

Audrey touched his arm. "She knows how important this is, she'll be here."

Jackson took her hand. "Come on. Angus needs the place to himself."

"Thank you," Angus said. "You've been great."

Audrey laid a protective hand over her belly. "I just don't want that bastard to ever threaten Gwen and her son again. And to think it's all because he needs the money for his gambling debt? What kind of lowlife threatens his own son?"

"We can discuss it in the storeroom," Jackson said,

his hand on the small of her back. "Let Angus handle this."

"I am. I just get all emotional."

"I know. It's all the baby hormones. Let me rub your back and anything else that might be aching."

"Jackson, you always know what's good for me." Audrey's voice faded as they disappeared into the storeroom.

The front door opened and Gwen appeared, blinking in the dim lights of the barroom. "Wayne?" she called out.

"Gwen, it's me." Angus hurried across the room and took her arm.

She jerked it free and backed a step, her face darkening. "I came here because Wayne said he had a solution and that you were involved."

"Good. I think we've got it nailed tight. If you'll have a seat over here, he'll be here any moment. I can explain everything to you later."

"There won't be a later. I'm going to say what I came to say to Wayne, and then I'm headed back to Dallas."

"Please stay long enough for me to tell you what's been going on."

"Oh, I know what's been going on, and I'm sorry to tell you that you're going to have to look elsewhere to satisfy your mother's ultimatum. I can't believe I fell for all that bullshit."

Angus's heart hit bottom, like a lead dumbbell in the pit of his belly. "Where did you hear that?"

"From the source. Your mother was practically cackling with glee that her son found a woman to marry and bear children. Well, you can take all your lies and shove them—"

"Gwendy! Angus!" Wayne appeared in the door. "I thought I heard you two in here. I can't stay long. I've arranged to meet with my…er…financial advisors at the truck stop in thirty minutes." He clapped his hands together. "I take it Angus explained everything to you?"

Gwen's eyes narrowed. "Explained what?"

Angus met Wayne halfway across the room and clapped a hand on his back. "I'm sorry. I didn't get a chance to talk to her like I thought I would. Perhaps you can explain the deal the way you explained it to me. Gwen is a reasonable businesswoman. I'm certain she'll be more than willing to help you out if you give it to her straight."

Wayne's brows dipped and he shot a cautious glance at Gwen and back to Angus. "Last time I talked to her about Dalton, she tossed me out of her room."

"And I'd do it again." Gwen's cheeks flew twin flags of red. "Why are you with Angus, and what deal are you talking about?"

"Angus said you'd changed your mind and would be open to making a deal concerning our son."

Angus prayed she'd at least hear him out before she tossed Wayne out the door again.

"For the twenty grand I need to pay off my debt, I'll sign over full custody of Dalton to you."

Gwen's nostrils flared. The only sign of her rage. "Twenty thousand dollars and you'll give up all rights to Dalton? You won't show up a year down the road, demanding visitation or more money to buy your way out of debt?"

He held up his hand. "I swear. Twenty thousand dollars and you'll never see me again."

"You'd sell your son for cold, hard cash?" Gwen closed her eyes. "I'm just glad I dropped Dalton off before coming here. He's better off thinking his father died in a car crash than to know the truth. His father's a deadbeat bastard who isn't worth twenty cents, much less twenty thousand dollars."

Gwen plunked her purse on the table and pulled out her checkbook. "I'll give you the twenty thousand, but I better never see you or your friend ever again." Her heart ached at the thought of Angus being a friend to Wayne. She wrote out the check and handed it to Wayne, shooting a killer look at Angus, her gaze sizzling a hole through his heart.

Damn. He should have known better than to leave Gwen with his mother. The woman would have been beyond ecstatic thinking she had one of her sons practically married off.

God, he wished he could have been in two places at once. But this meeting and everything that had gone into making it happen were too important to leave to chance. "Wait, Gwen." Where the hell was Sandy?

"Angus?" A female voice called out from the entrance to the Ugly Stick Saloon.

Angus's knees nearly gave in when he spied Sandy carrying her leather briefcase. Thank God. "Sandy, this is Wayne Kent and Gwendolyn Graves."

"You two are the biological parents of Dalton

Graves?" Sandy asked, setting the briefcase on a nearby table.

Gwen's shoulders pushed back and she lifted her chin. "I'm Dalton's mother. Who are you?"

"I'm your lawyer. Angus asked me to draw up papers to settle custody matters between you and your ex-husband."

Gwen glared at Angus. "I don't want your help, now or ever." She turned to Sandy. "I'm sorry you wasted your time. Now, if you'll excuse me, I have to go."

"Wait." Angus blocked her from leaving. "Hear her out. This will only take a minute and this will all be settled."

"Mr. Kent, I understand you've agreed to give up all custodial rights associated with the minor Dalton Graves."

"I do." He grinned, fanning his face with the freshly written check.

"Sign here." Sandy handed him a pen and a sheaf of papers and pointed to a line.

Wayne leaned over the papers. "What are these?"

"The legal documents signing over your rights." Sandy stepped back far enough so that he could glance over the document. "Please read through the wording carefully. Once you sign, it's done. You will have no legal claim on the minor."

"I don't need to read it. Just point to where you need me to sign and I'm out of here." Wayne gripped the pen, scribbling his signature and initials where Sandy indicated. When he was done, he straightened, holding the check in his hand. "That's it?"

"Just one more thing." Angus stepped up to him and plucked the check from Wayne's hand and ripped it in half.

"What the hell did you do that for?" Wayne wailed. "That was my money."

"Wayne, Wayne, Wayne," Angus said, shaking his head, "I did it for your own good. You didn't want to go to jail for blackmail, did you?"

Sandy tucked the papers into her briefcase and closed the lid. "I'll file these with the court tomorrow first thing." She held out her hand to Gwen. "Congratulations, you are the legal custodial parent of Dalton Graves."

Gwen took the woman's hand, her movements automatic, her face blank.

Once Sandy had left the saloon, Wayne pointed to Gwen's wallet. "Write another one, Gwendy baby." Wayne smiled at her. "Be a good girl, will ya?"

Her gaze steady, her lips firm, she said, "No. I'm finally, completely done with you, Wayne. Go away and never come back again."

"You can't do this. We made a deal."

Angus stepped between Wayne and Gwen. "No, you attempted to blackmail her. If you don't leave now, I'll have you arrested."

"You dirty, rotten bastard. Do you know what you've just done?"

He nodded. "Yes. I do. I protected the woman I love from a man who isn't fit to be in the same room with her or her son. Leave before I call the sheriff."

"I'll leave when I have the money and not a moment

sooner. Gwen, write that check or I'll never leave you or Dalton alone."

"Wayne, you don't have a case. Hell, you're lucky I'm not pressing charges. If you don't leave now, I will." She tilted her head. "Go."

Wayne's face flushed bright red. "Bastard." He swung a fist straight at Angus.

Angus sidestepped, grabbed Wayne's arm and yanked him around and clamped his arm around the bastard's neck. "You'd think you would have learned I don't mess around."

"You stupid son of a bitch. Those two men you pulled off me last night are waiting at the truck stop for their money. If I don't bring it, they'll find me, break my legs and leave me in a ditch to die."

Angus shrugged. "Should have thought about that before you spent their boss's money."

"I'll sue for custody."

Angus tightened his arm around the man's neck. "You just signed your rights away."

"I'll tell the judge I was under duress when I signed."

"Sandy will testify otherwise."

"And so will we." Jackson, Audrey and Libby appeared, forming a semicircle, backing Angus and Gwen.

Libby wiggled her fingers at Wayne. "Remember me? The bartender from last night? I remember you discussing wanting to trade custody of your son for twenty grand. I'll swear on a stack of Bibles in court to tell the truth, the whole truth and nothing but the truth." She smiled.

"Audrey and I stood just out of sight and heard everything you said today to Gwen about granting custody of your son for twenty thousand dollars. We'd gladly testify in court as to what we heard you say."

"You are not getting away with this." Wayne clawed at Angus's arm.

"I think we are." Gwen nodded toward the door. "You'd better get going if you want a head start to beat the loan sharks out of town." She glanced at her watch. "You don't have much time."

Wayne glared at her. "I should never have gotten involved with you."

Gwen's lip curled in a sneer. "I feel the same."

Angus escorted Wayne to the door and walked him outside.

GWEN GATHERED her purse and steeled her heart to leave Angus and Temptation forever.

Audrey, Jackson and Libby blocked her path before she could.

"Congratulations, Gwen. We're so happy for you." Audrey hugged her close, her baby bump a painful reminder of what could have been had Angus really cared for her.

Gwen's eyes burned and she fought to hold it together long enough to reach her car.

Jackson grinned. "Angus pulled all of this off between midnight last night and now. He was lucky to catch Sandy in town. She was here on vacation, visiting her parents. Thankfully, she had her laptop with the standard forms on it. Mona and Grant helped her with legal names, birthdates and addresses."

"It was pretty much a community effort," Libby said. "If Angus hadn't come in when he did last night, he wouldn't have come across Wayne being roughed up by his loan shark's goons. Wayne wouldn't have trusted him to set up this meeting and you wouldn't now have sole custody."

All because he didn't want to lose his ranch and his precious horses. She and Dalton meant nothing to him.

"Thank you all for helping make this happen." She slid her purse strap onto her shoulder. "But I really need to get back to Dallas."

She hoped Angus was still tied up with Wayne, and she wouldn't have to deal with him.

"Hey, take it easy on Angus. He's giving up a lot," Jackson called out after her.

Outside, a sheriff's cruiser idled in the middle of the parking lot. The deputy stood with Angus as Wayne drove away.

While their backs were to her, Gwen slipped by and climbed into her Cadillac, shifted into Drive and pulled away.

She refused to look in the rearview mirror, but a muffled shout made her heart clench. The sooner she collected Dalton and got out of town, the better. She pushed the accelerator to the floor, speeding down the highway, her eyes blurred with unshed tears.

As she reached the outskirts of Temptation, a siren alerted her to the emergency vehicle following her.

Gwen pulled to the side of the road and realized she

was the reason for the lights. She had no idea how fast she'd been going and really didn't care, as long as he wrote the damned ticket fast and let her go. The longer she remained stopped, the greater the chance that Angus would catch up to her, and she wasn't sure she could hold up to more of his lies.

God, she'd been an idiot to believe he really loved her and Dalton. Gwen slid the window down and waited for the lawman and her ticket.

The deputy got out of his vehicle and stepped up to her window. "Gwendolyn Graves?" he asked.

"Yes, sir."

"There's someone who'd like to talk to you before you get away." The deputy stepped back and Angus took his place.

He tried to open her door. "Gwen, we need to talk."

"I'm done talking." Despite her efforts to hold back, the tears slipped from her eyes. "Thank you for getting Wayne off my back. But I'm afraid I can't see you anymore."

"If this is about my mother's threat to sell the ranch, let me explain."

"You don't have to explain anything. You needed a wife. I was stupid enough to think you needed me. Well, I don't need you. And I won't let Dalton be a pawn in your bid to keep the ranch."

"Gwen, you don't understand."

"Oh, I understand all too well." Gwen shifted into gear and took off, leaving Angus standing on the side of the road in the flashing lights of the sheriff's cruiser.

Tears blinded her and she nearly missed her turn.

Sirens sounded again and she debated ignoring them and continuing on her course to Grant and Mona's. But the rule follower in her made her slow to a stop.

She slid her window down. "You're supposed to be a representative of the law. What reason do you have to pull me over this time?" she shouted.

The deputy stood to the side of her door. "Please step out of the vehicle."

"I'm not fuckin' believing this." She climbed out of the vehicle and glared at the deputy. "Where is he?"

"I don't know what you're talking about. Please hold out your hand."

"Why?" she asked, doing as she was told.

He snapped a handcuff on to her wrist. "Ma'am, I'm afraid I can't let you leave the county until you talk to my friend Angus McFarlan." The deputy held out the other end of the handcuffs.

Angus appeared and snapped the cuff on his own wrist. "Thanks, Dusty. I owe you one."

"Just don't tell the boss. He frowns on me arresting people for crimes of the heart." Dusty pointed a finger at Gwen. "Give the man a chance. He's one of the good guys." The deputy then climbed into his cruiser and drove away.

"He left!" Gwen tried to point her finger at the disappearing cruiser, but the movement brought Angus's hand with hers. "How are we supposed to get this thing off?"

"I guess we could follow him around on his shift until we catch up. But, first, I'd like to set a few things straight."

"Don't bother." Gwen turned to her car and waved a hand toward the interior. "You'll have to crawl across the console. I'm not."

Angus sighed. "I'll get in, but you're going to listen."

"Whatever." She waited for him to brush past her, his body touching her, sending a shock of electrical charges through her. He climbed across the driver's seat, in the process pulling her into the vehicle, sitting on the horn and knocking the shift out of gear. By the time Angus settled in the passenger seat, Gwen could swear she had a few bruises.

She shut her door and, with Angus's help, shifted into gear and drove to the hardware store.

"My mother's ultimatum had nothing to do with my feelings for you."

"Why don't I believe you?"

"Because you don't want to give me a chance. You're afraid to let yourself love me."

"I'm not afraid of loving you, because it's not going to happen. Once burned and all that…"

"Then tell me why you bought me at the auction, if deep down inside you didn't harbor some kind of hope that there was something still there?"

Her chest tightened and her gut twisted. "Dalton needed a role model."

"Bullshit."

"It's true. He needs a man to teach him how to play sports."

"You could have chosen any cowboy that night. But you chose me." He smiled. "And paid a lot of money for the privilege." His hand curled around hers, their cuffs clanking, metal on metal.

Gwen drifted to a halt at a stop sign, her eyes blurring again. She wanted to hate him for exposing her for the fraud she was, but he'd lied too. "You only went along with my dates because you needed a wife to appease your mother."

He shook his head. "No, I didn't."

"What other reason did you have? It's been seven years."

"I know. And I will forever regret that I didn't come after you. I thought you'd be better off without me and the ranch and all my responsibilities slowing you down."

"What if I wanted to be slowed down? You didn't even give me the choice." She shoved his hand away, but it only went so far before the chain binding them brought it up short. "You didn't come after me."

"I was hurt that you didn't tell me goodbye. I thought you had used me for a summer fling before going back to school. Even so, I was going to follow you to College Station the week after you left, but my mother was diagnosed with breast cancer. I couldn't leave her. Not when my father had died six months earlier, one brother was away at school and the other had left a year earlier and had yet to return for more than a day."

Gwen bit her bottom lip. "You had to stay and help your mother."

"By the time she made it through surgery and chemo, it was over a year. I looked for you in College

Station, but you'd moved and left no forwarding address. I realize now I should have kept looking. I didn't know you'd kept in touch with Mona."

"All that time." Gwen sat with her foot on the brake, her gaze staring out as if looking into the past.

"When you showed up at the Ugly Stick, I wasn't sure I wanted to start over with you. It hurt too much to lose you the first time. I loved you so very much and I still do."

"How can I believe you?" Gwen shook her head. "Of course you were happy I fell into your arms. If some poor girl hadn't come along, you stood to lose everything you'd worked so hard for. Land that has been in your family for over a hundred years, the breeding program you built from the ground up. Everything."

"I don't care about those things."

"Don't fill me full of more lies. You love those things."

A horn honked behind them.

Gwen realized she was still sitting at a stop sign and another vehicle had pulled up behind them. She pressed her foot to the accelerator and drove to a church parking lot and shifted into Park.

Angus captured her cheek with his unencumbered hand. "The ranch and the horses are things I can live without."

"Yeah, but you wouldn't have to if I went along with your plans."

"Gwen, will you listen?" He chuckled. "I'm selling my herd to Jackson."

"You're what?" She stared at him, her heart

thumping hard against her ribs. "Selling the horses you love?"

"I don't love my horses. I love you. I'm negotiating with Jackson Gray Wolf to purchase my breeding stock. Gwen, I'm selling out and moving to Dallas. I talked to my boss at the firm. They have an office they can put my name on. All I have to do is tell them when."

His words whirled around her but didn't want to stick. "But your mother's ultimatum."

"She can sell the damned ranch. I don't care about it. I care about you and Dalton. I have a feeling he and I are going to be great buds. If you let me become part of your life."

"But the ranch…" Gwen stared at Angus, her mouth hanging slack, "…how can you walk away from your family heritage?"

"Easy. If staying means losing you, I'd walk away from a hundred family ranches."

Her heart soared and she leaned across the console and caught his face between her palms. "You mean it?"

Angus grinned. "Every word."

She kissed him hard, her free hand circling the back of his neck to hold him closer, deepening their contact. When at last she broke free and sat back, breathing hard, she laughed out loud, feeling lighter, younger and more carefree than she'd felt in seven years.

"So, is there room in your and Dalton's lives for a cowboy without a ranch?" He held out his hands.

She laid hers in his. "Damn right there is. But if it's all the same to you, I don't want you to give up the ranch and the horses. They're a part of what makes you so special."

He winked. "I can be special without them."

"Dalton has such high hopes of you teaching him how to ride. And he wants his own pony and puppy. I can't keep a dog in Dallas. But I could commute a couple days a week."

"I could too. And I've always wanted to design and build my own house on the property."

"So does that mean I get the rest of my eight dates?" Gwen asked.

"That and so much more." Angus pulled her across the console and into his lap, kissing her soundly.

After several minutes, Gwen glanced up and noticed several cars pulling into the parking lot, their passengers glaring at them.

"Uh, sweetheart. It's Sunday."

Gwen laughed. "You think we'll go to hell for making out in the church parking lot?"

"If we are, let's make it good." Angus covered her mouth with his and gave the old ladies a good show.

Gwen laughed into his mouth and clung to him, promising herself she'd never let him go again.

*C*olin hit the last number and held his breath while the phone rang four times. He'd chosen to call using the phone at Molly's, knowing Brody wouldn't answer if he called from home.

On the fourth ring, someone picked up. "Hello."

"Brody McFarlan?" he asked.

"Yeah, who is this?"

His gut tightened. "Colin."

"What do you want?" His tone was flat, unemotional and a little annoyed.

Colin had rehearsed the entire conversation about how their mother had given them an ultimatum and demanded all three of them get their lives together, but with his brother's cranky tone, he didn't think he'd get halfway through his spiel before Brody hung up.

Instead, Colin said, "Mom's sick, maybe dying. You need to come home."

**If you enjoyed this book, try the other books in the
Ugly Stick Saloon Series**

Boots & Chaps (#1)
Boots & Sex Ed (#2)
Boots & Leather (#3)
Boots & Promises (#4)
Boots & Bareback (#5)
Boots & Dirty Tricks (#6)
Boots & Lace (#7)
Boots & Roses (#8)
Boots & Buckles (#9)
Boots & the Wishes (#10)
Boots & Twisters (#11)
Boots & the Bachelor (#12)
Boots & The Rogue (#13)
Boots & The Heartbreaker (#14)
Boots & Wings (#15)

BOOTS & THE ROGUE

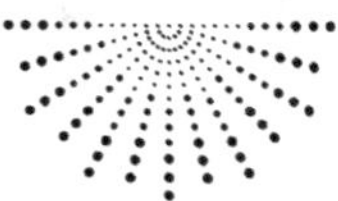

UGLY STICK SALOON SERIES BOOK #14

by Elle James
New York Times Bestselling Author

writing as

Myla Jackson

BOOTS
& the
ROGUE
UGLY STICK SALOON
New York Times Bestselling Author
ELLE JAMES
writing as
MYLA JACKSON

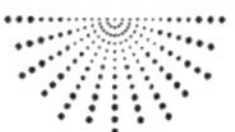

"Mom? Angus? I'm home!" Brody McFarlan pushed through the front door of the Rafter M Ranch main house. Stepping into the old colonial home was like stepping back into his childhood.

Nothing much had changed, other than a slightly different color of paint on the wall and maybe a new easy chair he hadn't noticed the last time he was there over a year ago.

"Mom?" he called out again, his heart bunching in his chest. Angus's and Colin's trucks weren't out front, and Brody hadn't driven around behind the house to see if his brothers had parked out by the barn. Damn. Had he arrived too late?

Pushing past the exhaustion of driving over twenty-five hours straight, he ran through the house, checking in his mother's bedroom and the kitchen. He was headed for the back door leading off the kitchen when it slammed open and a little boy of about five burst through, followed by a small golden retriever puppy with huge paws, yapping at his heels.

"You can't catch me!" the little boy shouted over his shoulder and barreled through the kitchen, slamming into Brody's legs.

The puppy sat back on his haunches in an attempt to stop, skidded across the wooden floor and bumped into the back of the little boy's knees, knocking him over.

Brody staggered backward, wondering if he'd wandered into the wrong house.

A female voice called from outside, "Dalton! Don't run in the house!" Seconds later, a gorgeous auburn-haired woman pushed through the door and stopped, her eyes rounded. "Oh, sorry. Can I help you?"

Brody stared at the boy and dog. "Do these belong to you?"

The woman laughed. "As a matter of fact, they do." She tilted her head and stared hard at him. "You look familiar."

"I'm sorry I can't say the same."

Her eyes rounded and she grinned. "You must be Brody." She leaned out the door. "Angus, sweetheart, come see who's here."

Heavy footsteps clunked against the wood planks of the deck outside and Brody's brother Angus filled the door behind the woman. He looped his arm around her waist and nuzzled her neck before he glanced up. "Who's here?"

When his gaze met Brody's he broke out in a huge smile. "Brody!"

The boy at Brody's feet stood and gathered the wiggling puppy in his arms. "Are you my Uncle Brody?"

"Well, actually—" the woman started but was cut off by more footsteps clomping against the deck.

"Angus! Gwen! Did you see which way Dalton and Shotgun went?" Brody's mother, Maggie McFarlan, burst through the door, her cheeks red, hair windblown and eyes sparkling. Far from the image Brody had in mind of a woman on the verge of death. "Oh, there he is. Thank goodness. I thought he might have gotten into the pen with the bull again." She glanced up and smiled. "Hello, Brody, it's good to see you." Then she blinked and the color drained from her face. "Brody?"

Brody nodded. "Hey, Mom."

Her eyes glistened with tears and she took a step toward him, then another and flung her arms around him, nearly tripping over the little boy at his feet. "Oh, Brody, I've missed you so much."

Brody hugged his mother long and hard. He had to swallow several times to loosen his constricted vocal cords. "I missed you too."

When he had a grip on his emotions, he held her at arm's length, scanning her face. "How are you? What does the doctor say? Why are you outside running around? Shouldn't you be in bed or in an easy chair resting?"

She frowned up at him and laughed. "What are you talking about? I'm fine."

More footsteps pounded across the deck outside the kitchen. "Hey, who left the door open on the chicken coop? There are chickens everywhere. I could use a hand getting them all back in the—" Colin, Brody's younger brother, banged through the door and came to a dead standstill.

Brody glared at him over his mother's head. "I drove twenty-five hours straight to get here."

"Oh, sweetheart." His mother cupped his cheek. "You must be exhausted."

"I am," he said through clenched teeth.

"Why didn't you take the usual three days?" she asked.

"Tell her." Brody's glare deepened.

Colin had the decency to blush. "Uh, could I get some help rounding up the chickens?"

Their mother frowned, her gaze shooting between Colin and Brody. "What's going on?"

Brody's anger simmered. "Colin called me exactly twenty-five hours ago to tell me you were sick, maybe dying. I dropped everything and came as fast as I could."

The little boy tugged on Brody's sleeve. "Are you my Uncle Brody?"

Brody looked down at the boy and back up to his mother and Angus. "Who are these people?"

Everyone talked at once until the cacophony of voices sounded like fans at a boxing match.

His head aching, his eyes burning from lack of sleep, Brody raised his hand and shouted, "Quiet!"

As if someone had turned the sound off on the radio, the kitchen got dead silent. Then the puppy in the boy's arms barked.

Angus took the dog from the boy and leaned in to hug Brody. "Hey, bro, glad you finally made it home. I'd like you to meet my girl, Gwen, and her boy, Dalton. The dog's name is Shotgun because he's fast out the barrel and scatters everywhere at once."

Gwen held out her hand. "Hello, Brody. Angus has told me so much about you. Well, about you as a boy growing up on the ranch. Nice to meet you."

Brody took her hand and shook it, his gaze going to Angus. "Your girl? Why didn't I know about this?"

"I'm sorry," his mother said. "It all happened so fast and I haven't talked to you in several weeks."

"You'd have known, if you'd been here," Colin said.

The silence stretched again.

"Well, now you are. Have a seat. Angus will make coffee, won't you, dear?" his mother said.

"What the h—" Brody glanced at the boy, and changed his expletive, "—heck is going on here?"

"Is Uncle Brody always mad?" Dalton asked, backing into Angus's legs, his eyes wide.

"No, Uncle Brody isn't always mad. Only for the last eight years," Colin said.

Angus shot him a killer look. "Mom, why don't you take Gwen and Dalton out and show them how to lead the chickens into the pen with a bucket of feed?"

"Oh boy!" Dalton ran for the door.

Mrs. McFarlan hooked Gwen's arm. "Come on, the boys need a little brotherly bonding time."

Colin snorted.

Their mother pointed at Colin and Brody. "Play nice and remember what I said." She shifted her gaze to include Angus and then stepped out the door.

Gwen shot a questioning glance at Angus and hustled Dalton out in front of her.

Once the women and the little boy were out of the house, Brody glared at his brothers. "What the hell is going on?"

"Sit." Angus pointed to the table.

Neither Colin nor Brody made a move to comply with his order.

Angus sighed. "Fine. Stand. But this might take a while to tell."

Colin broke in. "Mom's going to sell the ranch."

"What?" Brody looked from Colin back to Angus.

"Thanks, Colin." Angus shook his head. "Mom isn't selling the ranch; she's threatening to sell the ranch."

"Threatening?" Brody shook his head. "And you're sure she's not sick?"

"Cancer-free her last checkup. She's healthier than a horse."

Some of the tension Brody had carried with him from Seattle released. But this conversation was far from over. "Good. I'm glad she's doing better. But what did she mean by 'remember what I said'?"

Angus shoved a hand through his hair, standing it on end. "A couple weeks ago she told us that if the McFarlan men didn't show an interest in their inheritance, she was going to sell the Rafter M Ranch and everything on it."

"You and Colin have been here. I haven't. What's been going on to think you two aren't interested in the ranch?" Brody nodded toward Angus. "Aren't you raising horses and making a good go of it?"

Angus nodded. "Yeah, but that's not what she was talking about. She thinks there won't be any little McFarlans to pass the ranch down to."

"She wants us all married and having kids within two months. We're already down two weeks and have only six more to make it happen."

"What in the hell is he talking about?" Brody asked the oldest McFarlan brother.

"Just what Colin said—Mom wants us settled down, married or engaged by the end of the two months or she'll sell."

"Mrs. Reinhardt has been bragging about her grand-babies, and Mom is afraid she'll miss out unless she takes drastic measures," Colin inserted.

Angus nodded.

Brody stared at Angus. "Is that what Gwen and her boy are all about? Mom forced you into a relationship to save the ranch?"

"Yes…no…ah hell." Angus paced the length of the kitchen and back. "It started out that way."

Again, Colin jumped in with "Mom put my and Angus's name in the hat at the annual Ugly Stick Saloon bachelor auction. Gwen bought Angus for four dates and the rest is history."

Angus frowned at Colin. "Gwen and I knew each other seven years ago. I loved her then, but things didn't work out. The auction brought us back together." He smiled as he spoke. "I love Gwen and Dalton."

Brody was happy his brother had found a woman to share his life.

When Angus glanced up, his smile faded. "But we stand to lose the ranch if Mom's demands aren't met."

Brody crossed his arms. "And what does that have to do with me?"

"She wants all three of us married or on our way to being married within her two-month time frame. And she wants you home."

"Well, you got me home. But I'm not here to stay or to get married. I came because I thought Mom was sick." Again he threw another glare at Colin.

Colin pushed back his shoulders. "Would you have come if I'd asked?"

"Hell no."

"Would you have come if Angus had told you what was going on?" Colin continued.

Angus and Colin both stared at him, waiting for his answer.

"No," Brody said.

Colin's lips thinned and Angus's twisted in disappointment.

"This might not be home to you," Angus said, "but it's my home and I want to keep it."

"Mom is bluffing." Brody waved his hand at the kitchen with the copper-bottom pans his father had bought for their mother. She kept the copper polished and shiny. "She'd never sell the Rafter M. It has too many good memories of her life with Dad and us as kids growing up here. Hell, the place has been in our family for over a hundred years."

"One hundred fifty," Colin offered.

"I don't want to see it split up and sold, any more

than Colin does," Angus said. "I'm not sure what your job situation is—"

Brody held up his hand. "Don't even go there. I'm not staying."

Angus went on, "And I'm not asking you to stay forever, just stay long enough to get Mom to retract her ultimatum."

"I have a life in Seattle," he lied. He lived in Seattle, but he didn't know many more people in the big city than when he'd landed there eight years ago and found a temporary job as a bartender that he still worked part time while he pursued his second job, his real passion. "I can't hang around here until Mom changes her mind."

"At least stay until the end of the two months. Give Mom that. She loves you and wants to see you more often."

"She can come to Seattle. The road goes both ways."

"She wants you to come home," Angus insisted.

"What he means is Mom wants the two of us to kiss and make up," Colin finished.

Brody narrowed his eyes and stared at his younger brother. Because of Colin, he'd left home in the first place. Because his own brother betrayed him with the woman he was about to marry. He shook his head. "Not happening."

"Eight years is a long time to hold a grudge," Colin said. "I told you then I was sorry. What happened between me and Fancy shouldn't have, and I've regretted it ever since."

"You're damn right it shouldn't have happened."

Brody crossed to stand in front of Colin. "Who can you trust if you can't trust your own brother?"

Angus stared at Colin, a frown drawing his brows together. "You slept with Brody's fiancé?"

Colin's gaze never waivered from Brody's. "We didn't mean for it to happen. She was upset…one thing led to another…" He shook his head. "We shouldn't have done it, and we haven't seen each other since."

A long silence stretched between the brothers.

"Eight years, Brody," Angus finally said. "That's a long time. We're family."

Brody snorted. "That's what I thought, until my brother betrayed me."

Colin shook his head. "I told you it wouldn't do any good."

"Colin…" Angus pinned the youngest McFarlan with the same stern stare their father used on them when they were in trouble as children, "…would you go help the women."

Colin stood still for a moment longer, and then he turned and left the kitchen without another word.

"Whatever you have to say, I'm not listening. As soon as I've had a decent dinner and ten hours' sleep, I'm on the road back to Seattle."

Angus crossed the room and stood in front of Brody. "Fair enough." Then he hugged Brody hard. "I've missed you, brother."

When he stood back, the moisture in Angus's eyes could not be mistaken. That alone tugged hard at Brody's heart. "Two weeks. I'll stay for two weeks."

Angus nodded. "Thanks. Hopefully, within two

weeks we can talk Mom out of selling the ranch, and we can all get back to living our lives, drama-free."

That settled, Brody's stomach grumbled. "What I've missed is Mom's fried chicken. Do you think she'll cook that for dinner?"

Angus grimaced. "Oh, one other thing. As part of Mom's move-on-or-move-out ultimatum, she's on strike. She's not cooking, cleaning or buying groceries. We're on our own for food and laundry."

"You're kidding, right?"

"I wish I were." His face brightened. "I don't suppose you've picked up some cooking skills in your eight years on the West Coast?"

"I eat out all the time. I even burn toast." His stomach growled. "What do you do for dinner around here?"

"We eat at the diner in Temptation for the most part, but the Ugly Stick Saloon is having a barbeque tonight on account of the rodeo being in town. Gwen and Dalton are headed back to Dallas this afternoon. Mom's having dinner at Mrs. Reinhardt's. Colin and I were headed to the Ugly Stick. You're welcome to join us."

"I'm beat after being on the road."

"Man, there is nothing in the refrigerator."

His stomach grumbled again, making the decision for him. "The Ugly Stick Saloon it is."

"You're gonna love what the new owner has done to the place."

"Yeah?"

"She's a retired stripper married to Jackson Gray Wolf. They're about to have their first kid."

Brody's chest tightened. So much had changed at home. The Ugly Stick was under new ownership. His friend Jackson Gray Wolf had succumbed to the institution of marriage and his mother had gone off her rocker with crazy threats. He should have stayed in Seattle and forgotten Temptation, Texas, ever existed.

ABOUT THE AUTHOR

Twenty years of livin' and lovin' on a South Texas ranch raising horses, cattle, goats, ostriches and emus left an indelible impression on Myla Jackson, one she likes to instill in her red-hot stories. Myla pens wildly sexy, fun adventures of all genres including historical westerns, medieval tales, romantic suspense, contemporary romance and paranormal beasties of all shapes and sexy sizes. She lives in the tree-covered hills of Northwest Arkansas with her husband of more than 20 years and her muses—the human-wanna-be canines—Chewy and Sweetpea.

To learn more about Myla Jackson and her alter ego Elle James visit:

www.mylajackson.com

mylajackson@mylajackson.com

Honor Bound

Duty Bound

River Bound

Paranormal

Shewolf

Thorn's Kiss

Sex, Lies & Vampire Hunters